KU-716-658

Cast a Dark Shadow

Acclaimed army scout Wink Jefford finds himself put on trial for helping a captured Apache brave to escape from Fort Defiance in New Mexico. Forced to leave in disgrace, Wink is hired to guide some settlers to the town of Tularosa, but they are attacked by Apaches led by Mangus Voya, who is intent on driving the hated invaders from his lands.

Wink tries parleying with the Indians but is staked out. The wife of Mangus helps him to escape for saving her son, Shinto. On reaching Tularosa he is accused of cowardice for abandoning his duty, allowing the Indians to massacre the settlers. Wink is jailed by Sheriff Troy Vickery for his own safety. Shinto helps him to escape a lynching and reveals that the settlers were betrayed by a white man. Tracking down the culprit enables Wink to uncover the startling reason behind the treachery.

Cast A Dark Shadow

Ethan Flagg

A Black Horse Western

ROBERT HALE

© Ethan Flagg 2018
First published in Great Britain 2018

ISBN 978-0-7198-2793-8

The Crowood Press
The Stable Block
Crowood Lane
Ramsbury
Marlborough
Wiltshire SN8 2HR

www.bhwesterns.com

Robert Hale is an imprint
of The Crowood Press

The right of Ethan Flagg to be identified as
author of this work has been asserted by him
in accordance with the Copyright, Designs and
Patents Act 1988

All rights reserved. No part of this publication may be
reproduced or transmitted in any form or by any means,
electronic or mechanical, including photocopying, recording,
or any information storage and retrieval system, without
permission in writing from the publishers.

Typeset by
Derek Doyle & Associates, Shaw Heath
Printed and bound in Great Britain by
4Bind Ltd, Stevenage, SG1 2XT

ONE

THE ONLY GOOD INDIAN...

It was a blistering August day in the year 1875. A merciless sun blazed down from a cloudless sky of cobalt blue onto the heads of a new batch of recruits to B Company of the 4th Cavalry. The sweat-stained troopers were being put through their paces in the central square of Fort Defiance, New Mexico. Harried and castigated by a cold-hearted drill sergeant, they were being watched by a tall flaxen-haired army scout lounging on a chair beneath an overhanging veranda.

The buckskin-clad spectator had been hired as a civilian scout to tackle the recent uprising of the Mimbrano Apaches. Wink Jefford had only reached the fort earlier that day. A cigar in one hand and a bottle of cold beer in the other, the scout leaned back in his chair and emitted a deep sigh of satisfaction. He definitely had no wish to exchange places with the sweating recruits.

The tall rangy scout had been born Harvey Jefford. A deadly knife fight involving a Chiricahua Apache during the war against Cochise in Arizona left him with a lazy eye. The Indian came out of the tussle somewhat less fortunate and was soon heading for the happy hunting grounds. So Wink it had been ever since. Thankfully, the eye defect had in no way impeded his work as an army scout.

General Crook was now in charge of the operation to quell this latest Indian uprising led by a renegade chief, Mangus Voya. The general was due to arrive the following day with a full troop of cavalry. That gave Wink a rare opportunity to relax. And he was taking full advantage of it.

Mangus and his band of angry bucks were intent on sabotaging the peace being brokered by the authorities, and every day that passed he was gathering more rebels to the cause. The renegades were incensed that too many white settlers were invading their tribal lands. The hotheaded chief was a lone but influential figure whose depredations were likely to drag other restless tribes into the burgeoning conflict. A full-blown Indian war was the last thing the authorities needed, with new settlers now pouring into the southwest.

A new outpost sitting on an open plateau, Defiance had accordingly been well named. It had been thrown up quickly as a bulwark against attack to protect the incoming settlers. Crook knew that a swift response was essential to prevent an escalation of the conflict, but Mangus was a wily foe who knew the region much better than his enemies.

For the moment, however, Wink Jefford was free to pursue his own thing before the fireworks started. He puffed out a perfect smoke ring then imbibed a welcome drink of the cold beer. Although outwardly displaying a casual manner, Wink was concerned about the attitude of Defiance's current commander. His initial encounter with Colonel Dennison had made it abundantly clear that the guy hated Indians with a vengeance. The idea of making peace with these savages was anathema to his ethos. According to him, the only good Indian was a dead one.

Wink's crusty face wrinkled with disdain. Such an attitude could ruin the good work already negotiated with Guadalupe, the head honcho of the southern Apaches. He could only pray that the pragmatic General Crook would keep Dennison on a tight rein. At that moment, the double gates of the fort swung open and a patrol rode in. Wink's piercing blue eyes fastened onto the newcomers. Amidst the solid ranks of dusty blue, a downcast figure sat astride a pony. Head bowed and arms pinioned behind his back, he was clearly a captured prisoner. The scout's back stiffened. The headband securing long black hair put him down as a Mimbrano.

As the patrol trotted into the middle of the square, Wink was on his feet instantly. The cigar was tossed aside, the beer forgotten as his bulging eyes took heed of the captive's identity. 'What in blue blazes have you been doing to get yourself arrested?' he muttered under his breath.

The young brave was none other than Shinto, the son of Mangus. The scout knew that the youngster was under instruction by tribal elders for acceptance into full adulthood. Wink hustled across to where the patrol had come to a halt. 'What has the Indian been doing to get himself arrested?' he asked of the sergeant in charge.

'We caught him shooting deer with a bow and arrow,' the burly trooper replied, giving the prisoner a surly look of disdain.

'No harm in that, is there?' Wink replied, clearly puzzled by the arrest.

'Since the outbreak of the recent troubles, my orders are to bring in any bucks found off limits,' the sergeant retorted impatiently, recognizing the speaker as an army scout – an unnecessary interference, in his opinion. Hank Jenner had little time for civilians muscling in on matters of a military nature.

'I know for a fact that this particular one has been granted freedom to engage in tribal initiation tasks,' Wink insisted. 'It was agreed with Guadalupe himself.'

'You tell that to Colonel Dennison, mister,' the sergeant bit back, signalling for his men to drag the Indian off his horse. 'I'm just obeying orders.' He pushed Wink aside roughly. 'You men make sure the redskin is tethered to that post inside the guard tent while I report to the colonel.' As far as he was concerned, the cranky confab was closed.

Grave concern registered on Wink's tight features. If Mangus heard about this, he shuddered to think what the outcome would be. At the very least it would stir up the renegades even more than they were now. He waited for the sergeant to make his report and leave before Wink headed across to the commanding officer's quarters. A corporal barred his way when he tried barging into the office. 'Have you an appointment to see the colonel?' the lackey enquired snootily. 'He has given orders not to be disturbed.'

'He'll sure want to hear what I have to say,' Wink pressed, holding the man with a fervent glare. In truth he knew the exact opposite would likely be the case. The scout's cogent insistence, however, found the clerk delivering the demand for a hearing. Following a brief interlude, a surly grunt from behind the closed door saw the scout being ushered into the hallowed sanctum.

'Something I can do for you, Jefford?' The officer's brusque query was clipped and formal. 'With General Crook due any day, I'm busy, so make it quick.'

'It's about the arrest of Shinto,' Wink began, trying to maintain a steady and even delivery to his request. 'What do you intend doing with him?'

The starchy officer looked up from the documents he had been studying. His thick rubbery lips quivered with unconcealed disdain as he wrapped them around a glass of whisky. He also had little regard for civilian army scouts. 'If'n its any business of your'n, I intend putting him on trial for murder. There have been a couple of unexplained settler deaths in recent weeks. And I reckon those renegades are at the bottom of it.'

His words were slurred. The bottle was almost empty. It appeared to Wink as if the hard liquor had influenced the commander's bellicose manner, but the high-handed attitude induced a correspondingly stiff response.

'That young brave isn't to blame,' the scout protested, his natural instinct for justice bubbling over. 'He's under tribal instruction. No good can come of keeping him prisoner. It will only stir the Indians up. This is our one big opportunity to secure a lasting peace with the Apaches. What you are doing will ruin everything.'

Dennison jumped to his feet and slammed a bunched fist down onto the desktop. The whisky spilling across the desk went unheeded. 'Don't tell me how to run this fort. I've been hunting down Indians my entire military career. Those red devils are nothing but trouble and need exterminating. If'n you have a beef, take it up with General Crook. But I can tell you now that he always backs the decisions made by senior officers. So if'n that's all, I have work to do.'

As far as the martinet was concerned, the incident was closed. Wink struggled to keep his temper under control. But he knew that with an Indian-hater like Dennison, no amount of logic would prevail. All he could do was throw an impotent glare at the officer's bowed head.

10

He left, tossing back an ominous prediction. 'You're gonna regret this, Colonel.' There was no response from the obdurate commander. Wink knew full well that Mangus would not sit idly by and allow his son to likely face a firing squad. He was under no illusions that the irascible commandant would demand such a punishment. There was only one solution.

What he had in mind went against all of Wink's rationale. It was a blatant disregard for army law, but he felt there was no other way out of this dilemma. He would have to contrive the release of the brave. After giving it some serious thought the decision was made. But such action could not be undertaken before darkness enclosed the fort in its pitchy embrace.

TWO

. . . IS ONE RESCUED

The next few hours found the scout working out a plan of action. Due to the fort being newly built, no cellblock had yet been constructed. Any prisoners were tethered to stakes that had been driven into the ground inside a tent. Wink held off until the moon drifted behind a bank of cloud. Checking the guard was on the far side, he sneaked over to where Shinto was confined and slit a hole in the canvas with his knife.

Surprised by this unexpected entry to his prison, Shinto turned his noble head. Wink placed a finger over his lips. 'Make no noise,' he whispered. 'I am here to save you.' He then crawled in through the narrow opening, cutting the leather holding straps quickly. 'Your horse is ready outside. Put these on to make the guard think you are going out with me on patrol.' He handed over a greatcoat and trooper's wide-brimmed blue hat. 'Push your hair up into the crown.'

All the while, he kept a sharp eye open through the front aperture for any sign that the skulduggery had been sussed. The guard's attention remained focused in the opposite direction. A brisk gesture indicated the young Indian to follow him out of the torn hole. 'Why you do this, white man?' the Indian hissed, nonplussed by this sudden change in his fortunes. 'My father says that all white eyes are bad and should not be trusted.'

'Well, you can tell him that you have met one who doesn't think that way. And he has proved it by saving you from a firing squad.' He urged the Indian to don the stolen items. 'Hopefully, this disguise will fool the sentry on the gate long enough for you to escape.'

The two mounted up. 'Let me do all the talking. And keep your hat pulled low.' Sucking in a deep breath, Wink then led the way over to the main gate.

'Halt! Who goes there?' The challenge from the sentry was brittle and accompanied by a raised Spencer.

'It's me, Wink Jefford. I'm the new scout. Me and my partner are heading out to check the coast is clear for when General Crook arrives tomorrow.'

The sentry was sceptical. 'Bit late to be going out, ain't it?'

'An army scout's work don't keep to regular hours.' He hawked out a nervous guffaw. 'We won't be gone more'n a couple of hours.'

'Guess it's all right, then,' the man replied, drawing back the heavy latch and pulling open the gate. 'Watch yourself. Those redskins don't keep regular hours, neither.' Wink nodded as he passed the sentry, making sure his associate was on the far side hidden from close scrutiny.

They had only just exited the fort when a sudden gust of wind blew the hat off Shinto's head. His long black hair fanned out. The game was up. The vigilant sentry emitted a startled explanation of surprise. 'What the heck! The Indian's escaping!' he shouted. 'Call out the guard!'

The man raised his rifle, aiming it at the escaping Indian. Wink quickly nudged his horse into the man, knocking him off balance. The bullet whistled harmlessly into the air. But the manoeuvre had unsettled the animal, which skittered and whinnied. Shinto was able to make good his escape, but his liberator was left facing half a dozen rifles, all aimed his way. 'The scout has helped the Indian prisoner to escape. Grab him!' shouted the guard, keeping his rifle steady.

More troopers were arriving. They secured the wrongdoer roughly, but not before a few punches were thrown; Wink's reaction was to fight back. But the writing was on the wall. He stood no chance and was soon brought to the ground. Boots slammed into his ribs until an officer arrived to bring some order to the mêlée.

'What's this ruckus all about?' he demanded as the

men dragged the bruised scout to his feet quickly.

'This man has assisted a prisoner to escape, sir,' Sergeant Jenner replied, having put the boot in too. 'We captured an Apache buck and brought him in as ordered. This guy expressed his reservations to me but I told him to take it up with the Colonel. But I didn't figure he'd pull a stunt like this.'

'You're in deep trouble, Jefford. Helping a prisoner to escape, especially an Apache, is a court martial offence,' the young officer espoused. 'Colonel Dennison will throw the book at you. Bring him along, Sergeant.'

Wink was taken before the commanding officer, who had to be roused from his bed. The Colonel was not best pleased at being disturbed. Two troopers on either side held the prisoner firmly as Dennison berated him loudly. 'I knew you were a damned Indian-lover, Jefford. But I never figured you for a traitor.' The Colonel clenched his fists. All his instincts screamed out to physically attack the prisoner. A lifetime living and working under the rule of military discipline, however, held him in check. 'You will be court-martialled tomorrow when General Crook arrives, and I will be urging him to have you shot for this despicable crime.'

A spirited attempt to explain his reasons for the desperate action was cut short by Dennison. 'I am not interested in your excuses. We're at war, Jefford. The army will not tolerate disloyalty of this sort from anybody. Shackle him to the open air holding post, Sergeant. And this time post a double guard.'

Unfortunately for the pinioned captive, that night delivered a sharp thunderstorm. The heavens emptied and he was soon drenched to the skin. It was a miserable period for the doughty scout, whose resolute fortitude was strained to the limit. How had his life come down to this? Chained like a common brigand for trying to prevent war breaking out. Questions buzzed through his head. Had he done the right thing in helping Shinto escape, or had he merely exacerbated the problem?

Normally able to catch forty winks in any situation, little sleep was possible under such trying circumstances. It was accordingly with mixed feelings that he greeted the dawn chorus as Fort Defiance came awake. Thankfully the storm had abated; the warmth of the new day's sun was a welcome distraction from ugly thoughts of what the day would bring. Would it be his last on this earth?

Time passed slowly as the fort went about its daily business. The tethered scout was given a wide berth, everybody heedful of the coming court-martial when General Crook arrived. Soon after the noon hour, the renowned Indian fighter entered the main gate at the head of his men. The scout watched closely as he was greeted by Colonel Dennison, who led him into the headquarters building immediately. No doubt talk was brought round quickly to the problem posed by Wink Jefford.

And so it proved. Within the hour a table was set up outside with three officers in attendance: General Crook flanked by Colonel Dennison and a young

16

subaltern introduced as Lieutenant Isaac Dennison, the commanding officer's son, newly arrived at the fort with the General. Wink noted ominously that he was a carbon copy of his father. A pitiless sneer indicated he also held the same rigid viewpoint.

The outcome of this tribunal did not bode well for the prisoner. Released from the holding post, Sergeant Jenner and two guards frogmarched him over to the hastily convened tribunal. 'Prisoner will stand to attention,' the sergeant ordered.

Wink presented a sorry sight as he waited for the proceedings to commence with a doleful heart. Lank hair like rats' tails hung down over his ashen face. Dennison's grim expression gave no hint of any mercy being shown.

It was General Crook who opened the proceedings, outlining the charge against the prisoner, who was being tried under the precepts of military law. Once the preliminaries were delivered, he softened his tone momentarily with a personal statement. 'I've known you for a long time, Jefford,' he declared, leaning forward. 'We have been through many tricky situations together and I have always held you in the highest regard as a scout for the army.' Wink's mood lightened; hope flared.

But it was all a chimera. The benevolent manner was replaced by a harder, more authoritarian tone. Crook's brow furrowed with disappointment. A modicum of regret was replaced by a stoical determination to see the law upheld. 'You've let me down, Wink. Assisting the escape of a captive is a serious matter. But this tribunal does give you the opportunity to explain your actions.'

Wink sucked in a deep breath as the court, and indeed all of Fort Defiance, waited. He did his best to clarify his reasoning. But the cold regard aimed his way did not bode well for his chances. At least they had the courtesy to hear him out. Following the termination of the evidence from those involved, the captain in charge of the proceedings announced, 'The court will now retire to consider its verdict.'

Fifteen minutes later they returned for General Crook to deliver the judgment. He locked eyes with the prisoner, the tight-lipped expression displaying little in the way of clemency. Dennison, together with his son, were looking none too happy with the way things had gone inside the office. Again, Wink's downcast mood lightened. Perhaps he was to be exonerated. But that proved to be a fantasy as the General delivered his final assessment.

'Whatever your reasons for releasing a prisoner, you must appreciate that the army cannot condone any kind of vigilante action. As a military scout you have a duty to follow orders and not take the law into your own hands. Had you accepted the situation, I might well have sympathized with your viewpoint. But acting alone in this manner will not be tolerated. Accordingly, you are to be stripped of your honorary lieutenant's rank and henceforth removed from active service.'

Dennison couldn't resist cutting in with a bitter piece of invective. 'If'n the court had accepted my proposition you would have been up before a firing squad for aiding and abetting the enemy. Think yourself darned lucky to escape this easily.'

'That's enough, Colonel,' Crook snapped. 'The court has decided and my judgement is final. The commanding officer's request would certainly have been on the cards had you been an enlisted man. As it is, we do not have the authority to pass capital judgement on civilian personnel. Get your things together and leave the post immediately. The case is closed.'

A look of regret passed between the two men before the general stood up and turned away. The prisoner's bonds were released and he suddenly found himself alone, a pariah, shunned by those he had considered close colleagues. Nobody wanted to be seen associating with the shamed scout. There was nothing more for it but to leave as quickly as possible.

Jeers greeted the scout as he left Fort Defiance through the main gate. Wink couldn't really blame them. Indian fighting was a tough and often brutal business. Perhaps the general was right: he ought to have raised the matter with him personally. He shrugged. No point now in crying over split milk.

THREE

. . . AND YET AGAIN!

It was with mixed feelings that Wink Jefford left the army post behind. Jobless and with this accusation hanging over his head, he mused ruefully on what the future had in store for him. The lazy eye flickered with uncertainty.

When things had gone awry on previous occasions, Wink had sought out the nearest wilderness to be alone. On leaving Defiance, the Capitan Mountains offered the peace and tranquillity he badly needed. Being exiled in dishonour like some treacherous Judas did not sit well with the once-eminent scout. It was a bitter pill to swallow. A battle fought inside his head struggled with the conviction that he had done the right thing by releasing Shinto, but look where it had got him: ostracized by his own kind.

He sat his horse, allowing Patch to pick his own route across the level plateau while brooding on the fickle trick fate had played on him. A chirping flight of meadowlarks went unheeded. Even the squawking from a galloping roadrunner failed to raise a smile.

He left the main trail, meandering up into the Capitan foothills. Communing with nature in the raw always helped to settle his mind. Wink followed a narrow deer run up through the pine-clad slopes, struggling to erase the distraught events of recent days from his mind. On all sides surging peaks bristled for attention, the highest sparkling white with ice. Sparkling, clear air filled his lungs, deep breaths of which helped erase the pain of an unwarranted dishonour.

A little hunting and fishing in lonely creeks well removed from human interference ought to clear his mind. High up in the remote wilderness of the Capitans he could purge his soul. A secluded upland valley was the ideal panacea.

He had soon constructed a bivouac and settled down that first night staring into the embers of a fire while chewing on the sinewy leg of a burnt rabbit. It tasted perfect. With hot coffee and a cigar to finish, he settled down under a blanket of twinkling stars, with only the occasional night callings to disturb a blissful sleep.

Time and the isolation indeed proved to be great healers. A week later he felt revitalized, convinced he had done the right thing in helping Shinto escape. Wink Jefford was now ready to resume his life.

Leaving the unspoilt utopia of the hidden valley, he headed down through narrow gorges into the Ruidoso Downs. Another day found him crossing the Lincoln plateau, and beyond that laid the town of Carrizozo.

It was here that Wink hoped to secure a post guiding settlers into the newly opened territory to the west. And with Mangus on the rampage, he was certain his services would be welcomed. Before joining the army as a scout, Wink had earned a solid reputation leading numerous wagon trains to the promised land of Oregon along that famed trail.

On nearing Carrizozo, he spotted a line of the white-topped prairie schooners on the edge of town. No time like the present for checking if they already had a guide. He quickly picked out the leader of the group, a stocky jasper issuing orders in a curt voice that carried on the light breeze.

He waited for the man to finish before approaching him. 'I was wondering if'n you'd taken on a guide yet,' he began, having caught the man's attention. 'Mangus Voya has broken out of the reservation and is on the warpath. I can ensure you get through unscathed.'

The wagon master looked the newcomer up and down before replying. He nodded slowly. This guy sure had the look of a scout. 'I heard tell that red devil was on the prod. Maybe we could use a guide who knows the territory. You have any experience in scouting?'

'I sure have,' Wink replied eagerly. 'Led many a

22

train through to Oregon before I headed south into New Mexico.'

The man was impressed. 'I was wondering how best to reach Magdalena without getting attacked. Seems like you've moseyed by at just the right time. The name's Hake Windthrop. I'm the wagon master.' He held out a hand, raised eyebrows indicating for the new scout to likewise identify himself.

'Glad to meet you, Hake. I'm Wink Jefford.'

Instantly, the hand was withdrawn. The hospitable smile disappeared, being replaced by a snarled grimace. 'Jefford, eh? I've heard all about you getting thrown out of Fort Defiance for releasing one of those murdering redskins. I don't cotton to critters that double-cross their own kind.'

Wink was stunned into silence. He hadn't figured that news of his ignominious removal would have filtered down the grapevine so fast. There again, bad news always did travel quicker than the good sort.

'Your kind ain't welcome in Carrizozo,' Windthrop rasped. 'I'll find me a guide someplace else; someone I can trust. And definitely not a darned Indian-lover.'

The wagon master deliberately turned his back on the scout and walked away, leaving Wink stunned, and once again isolated and alone. But this time it was of a far more unsettling nature. The discourse had not passed unnoticed. Accusatory eyes followed the scout as he mounted up.

A kid threw a stone that struck Patch on the neck. The horse whinnied, rearing up and threatening to unseat his rider. Wink struggled to bring the faithful stallion under control. Another hard missile hit him on the back. Shouts and taunts threatened to escalate into a violent assault.

'And don't come back. . . .' was the final blurred command from Hake Windthrop as the dazed victim escaped with nothing more than his pride injured. But pride is a hard taskmaster to satisfy: one that a man used to high esteem found difficult to swallow. All he could do was put some distance behind him and hope that news of his humiliation was confined to the limited area of the Capitan Valley. This was clearly no place to linger. He urged the horse to a gallop, only slowing down on the edge of the town.

The last abode on the edge of Carrizozo was a pig farm run by a grizzled old jasper. He waved the rider to a halt. 'I heard the commotion those folks were making. Clearly none of them has ever worn the uniform. You won't know me, but I sure recall your exploits against Geronimo. We'd all have fallen foul of that critter if'n you hadn't suspected that ambush he set at Tomahawk Gap.'

'Sure, I remember that,' Wink recalled. 'He was a wily cuss, all right. But I couldn't help but respect him for trying to defend what he felt was right.'

'I finished my time last year in the cookhouse at Fort Singleton on the Gila River. Bought me some pigs and settled down here. Done well for myself, too.' A hand casually wafted over the holding, where upwards of two dozen porkers were snuffling in the dirt. 'You can't go wrong with bacon.'

Wink grinned. 'Can't say that I disagree with you there. Beans just don't sit right on a man's stomach without a good slice.'

'Enough of my history,' the old soldier concurred, hurrying on. 'The reason I stopped you was to say that a group of wagons broke from the main train and left here three days since. Windthrop urged them to stick with the main body for protection, but their leader was a stubborn jasper who said they were headed for Tularosa by the quickest route. They headed due south from here.'

'That would see them heading into the *Yermo Tierra* – that's one mean desert.' Wink mused, his rugged features tightening with concern.

'That's what Windthrop said, but that fella was adamant there was a short cut.' The old soldier shook his head of unruly grey curls. 'I've never heard of one that wagons can pass through. My guess is they could sure use the experience of a good scout to set them on the right trail.'

'I'm obliged to you, Mister. . . ?'

'Just call me Bacongrease, like everyone else does.' He paused to reflect, pulling out a corncob pipe and sticking it between yellow stumps of teeth. 'Reckon you must have had good reason for what you did at Defiance. Now go sort those folks out.'

Wink smiled down at the mud-smeared pig breeder and tipped his hat. 'Much obliged for the tip, Bacongrease. Each time I tuck into a good breakfast in future, I'll be thinking of where it came from.' And with that, he continued on his way. Squared shoulders and a fresh twinkle in his eye were communicated to the high-stepping appaloosa. This bright mood of optimism had been put there by an old veteran who had displayed some faith in him.

Wink Jefford, now an ex-army scout, had much to think on as he cantered off, heading in the direction indicated by Bacongrease.

Ruts scored by passing wagons indicated the trail had been well used by incoming settlers. But how many would reach their destination unimpeded by the incensed Apaches? That dilemma was now in the lap of the gods.

Not that Wink could rightly blame Mangus. This land had once been the sole preserve of his people. Now these invaders were taking it away. Little wonder they saw themselves as victims and had rebelled against anybody seeking to steal their heritage. But wholesale killing was not the answer. The American frontier was expanding at an alarming rate and nothing would stop it. Power was now in the hands of the white immigrants eager to settle this untamed land. The tribes would have to accept that such progress was inevitable. But the whites had a responsibility to make the change palatable. At some point there would have to be a compromise if more bloodshed was to be avoided.

To intercept the wayward settlers, Wink left the main trail, crossing an arid wasteland of shifting sand and stunted Joshua trees. This strange relation of the yucca was reputed to have been named after a biblical character by monks accompanying Spanish *conquistadors* in the 16th century. The spreading branches gave the impression of arms raised in thankful glory to Heaven for Joshua's capture of Jericho. The white invaders were equally pleased with their own subjugation of the New World.

Hat pulled low to shield his eyes from the sun's harsh glare, Wink peered up at the surrounding ramparts of fractured rock to his left. This was ideal terrain to conceal Mangus and his rebellious followers. A shiver ran through the taut frame. Any wagons caught out here would be sitting ducks. He pushed on quickly. This was no place to linger.

It was around noon that his sharp eyes spotted a line of tracks crossing his trail. He frowned, puzzled by the presence of unshod hoof prints in the sand. Only Indians rode such mounts. This was just one horse and it was walking. Nevertheless, his whole body stiffened. Where there was one, others would follow. A rapid scan of the terrain revealed that, for the moment at least, he was alone.

Cautiously, he followed the tracks. A half hour later he came across what had clearly been a flurry of movement in the sand. Nobody was around, so Wink stepped down, crouching to tease out what it all meant. An experienced scout's intuition now kicked in when he spotted the alien intrusion. His eyes widened. What was a shod horse doing mixing it with an Indian pony? Walking towards the edge of the jumbled prints, he came across a set of human indentations made by a pair of Indian moccasins. More sinister were the dark stains accompanying the line.

Blood! A fracas had taken place and the Indian had clearly come off worst. He paused, searching eyes tracing the path of the dragged feet as he followed warily. And there, a short distance ahead, he espied the adverse result of the attack. Narrowing his gaze, the scout led his own horse towards what looked like a leg half-concealed by the bulky trunk of a Joshua tree. The still form was approached with infinite care, the trusty .44 Colt Frontier gripped tightly ready for instant use.

An unforeseen jolt gripped the scout as he stepped round the tree. There, lying prone on his stomach, was none other than Shinto. The young brave whom he had helped escape from Fort Defiance had clearly not reached his father's camp. His eyes were closed. Wink carefully eased the young Indian over. The bullet in his shoulder was not life threatening, but was leaking too much blood. Stuck out here with his life force draining into the desert sand did not bode well for the Indian.

Wink stepped back, his eyes searching the immediate surroundings for any sign that the gunman was still around. It appeared that he had vamoosed. Shinto needed help if he was to survive, but the only medic available was back in Carrizozo.

A hesitant sigh issued from between gritted teeth. Wink was no sawbones, but would have to perform the surgical procedure himself for Shinto to reach adulthood. He uncorked the canteen, dribbling the life-giving elixir down the boy's parched throat. But it appeared that Shinto had been playing possum.

28

The wily kid must have sensed the presence of the newcomer and now reared up, intent on sticking the deadly blade clutched in his right hand into the stomach of his saviour.

Any other man but Wink Jefford might well have been gutted there and then. But the tough scout had not survived numerous clashes with both white and red foes without acquiring a marked degree of cunning to outwit such devious tactics. His hand shot out gripping the knife arm, twisting it from the weakened grasp. He tossed it aside wrestling the Indian back down onto his back.

'What in tarnation you trying to pull?' he snapped. 'Can't you see when a guy's trying to save your danged hide?'

Shinto struggled to free himself, but in his condition was no match for the wiry scout. 'A white man did this and left me here for dead.' Shinto spat into the dust as he sank back, exhausted. 'Why else would you have returned if not to finish the job?' He was breathing heavily. An angry scowl creased the pain-filled expression. 'Just do your worst so that I, Shinto, can join my ancestors lodging with the Great Spirit. My father was right. All white men are cursed dogs.'

'Look at me, you young pup,' Wink replied tartly. 'I'm the fella what helped you escape from Fort Defiance. Here I am, having lost my job because of it, and once again doing a good deed. And all I get is you trying to hook out my guts. I ought to grant your wish and leave you here for the buzzards.'

Shinto's eyes widened. He stared hard into the

eyes of his saviour, gripping Wink's arm tightly. 'Forgive me, white man. I did not recognize you.' The anger dissolved quickly, replaced by a shamed droop of the mouth. He then fell back, his breathing shallow and laboured, the effort draining what little strength remained. The last piece in the puzzle now slotted home. Wink surmised that the assailant had spotted him and ridden off, taking Shinto's horse and leaving the poor kid to bleed out his life under the harsh desert sun.

'Looks like I saved your hair just in time,' he remarked, cutting open the Indian's shirt, which invoked a pained grimace. 'That skunk must have been after your scalp. Indian hair fetches ten dollars a time.' He spat in the sand, displaying his abhorrence for the gruesome practice. 'Did you get a look at who shot you?' he asked. Shinto shook his head. 'Seems like the skunk must have heard me coming and skedaddled,' Wink continued. 'Typical bushwhacker. At least I deprived the rat of his conquest.'

He turned his attention back to the injury. The bullet was lodged under the collarbone at the rear and would have to be dug out soon to prevent infection setting in. He lit a match under the blade of his own knife in a perfunctory attempt at sanitization. It was the best he could do under the circumstances. The patient's leather headband was then stuck between his teeth. 'Bite down hard. This is gonna hurt some.' Shinto's face remained inscrutable. The kid was one tough cookie.

Wink then set to work. This was not the first bullet

he had dug out. Shinto's body stiffened as the blade bit deep, searching for the hidden hunk of metal. Yet no sound escaped through his strained mouth as the crude operation progressed. Luckily the bullet was not too deep, and within five minutes it had been extracted, but the wound needed cauterizing. Wink broke open one of his cartridges and poured some of the powder into the ragged lesion. He lit a match. Shinto's eyes widened. 'Best bite down hard, buddy. Ain't no sidetracking this if'n you want to reach old age.'

The powder sizzled and spat as it burned, sealing the edges of the wound. The Indian gritted his teeth. Fingers clawing at the sand was the only sign he was experiencing great pain. Yet throughout the fiery torment he never uttered a sound.

Wink could not help but admire the young brave's courage. 'Mangus should be proud to have a son like you,' he said, using his own bandanna to clean the wound as best he could, fastening it tight with strips from the Indian's shirt. 'That should stop any more bleeding,' he said wiping the gory knife on his own stained buckskin trousers. 'But you're gonna need a real sawbones to ensure it heals up good.'

Shinto's gratitude showed in his eyes. 'You must go now,' he urged the rough and ready surgeon. 'My father will be searching for me. He will have heard the shot. If he finds you here, there is no telling how he will react. His heart is set on complete annihilation of the hated invaders.'

'Guess you're right there,' Wink concurred rising

31

to his feet. He handed over the .36 Navy lead ball that had been extracted. 'Keep this as a reminder, proving that one white man at least has no truck with Colonel Dennison's belief that the only good Indian is a dead one.'

Hawkish eyes swept the surrounding line of hills constantly as Wink rode off. Now he had to keep a weather eye open for the scalp-hunter as well the renegade Mimbrenos. Only when he left the hill country behind and was crossing the level sward of flats known as the White Sands did he feel able to relax. There was no way he could be taken by surprise out here. Only isolated clumps of creosote bush and mesquite disturbed the endless belt of constantly shifting dunes. Most prominent, however, were numerous examples of the tall yucca that sprouted yellow flowers during the growing season.

FOUR

WAGON TRAIN

It was the following day when a low dust cloud broke over the rolling horizon. Of itself, such a phenomenon was nothing to cause alarm except for the fact that no breeze was astir to whip the sands into motion. This had to be of human origin. Wink's acute senses assumed instantly that Mangus Voya had somehow outflanked him during the night.

He waited a full ten minutes behind some yuccas before the alien intrusion slowly resolved itself into a small wagon train. One man riding fifty yards in front had to be the leader of the outfit that comprised four Conestogas. A small bunch of cattle could be seen trundling behind, urged on by a drag rider. The watcher could breath easier once again. At least he had located the wayward settlers. Although what these jaspers were doing out here in the wilderness of White Sands was anybody's guess. They ought to have been well to the west of here.

He spurred his horse to intercept the party. The leader raised a hand to halt the wagons on catching sight of the approaching figure. The wagon master was eyeing the newcomer with open suspicion. His hand rested on the Manhattan five-shot .31 Navy stuck in his belt. 'Some'n we can do for you, mister?' was the surly response from a well-built man in his middle years. Grey wisps of straggly hair poked below a shabby felt Stetson that had lost all its shape. His clothes were coated in a thick layer of white dust.

Wink kept his hands low, holding the reins. 'I was wondering what you folks were doing way out here,' he replied. 'You're a long way off the regular trail if'n Tularosa is your destination.'

The man ignored the enquiry, his mistrust heightened. 'How did you know where we were headed?' he rasped. 'And what business is it of your'n, anyway?'

'Easy there, mister,' Wink espoused, hoping to pacify the niggling doubts this mulish jigger was harbouring. 'Just a friendly enquiry from a passing traveller just out of Carrizozo. Word was that a group of wagons were headed that way.'

The wagon master huffed some but relaxed his stiff posture somewhat. 'We split from the main body of settlers 'cos they weren't going our way,' he declared firmly. 'My aim is to reach Tularosa in the next couple of days. I'm going to join my younger brother to run a cattle ranch on some land I've bought.'

Wink gave the man's claim a look of bleak scepticism. 'In that case, you're headed in the wrong direction,' he averred, shaking his head. 'Carry on this way and those wagons will end up bogged down in soft sand. The nearest waterhole is a good week's travel at wagon speed in the other direction. You folks should have headed south after passing Bodkin Butte.'

The wagon master removed his hat scratching his matted hair in frustration. 'I was getting a mite worried when we never found any water,' he said, grateful to share his concerns with a helpful stranger. 'The barrels are almost dry and we have two women on board. The cattle have been bawling as well.' He eyed the newcomer with renewed hope as a notion occurred to him. 'You seem to know this country pretty well, mister. How would you feel about taking over and leading us out of this mess? I'll pay you for your time,' he beseeched, pleading eyes desperately entreating the newcomer to help him out.

Wink was taken aback by the fervent request. After his knock back from Hake Windthrop in Carrizozo, he hadn't expected the guy described by Bacongrease to be so eager for any help. This guy's suggestion found him musing silently. Now it had come down to the crunch though: did he really want to be responsible for the welfare of these folks? Not particularly.

Accepting this job would be vastly different to guiding wagons over an established route. That said, he needed to find work now he was finished with the military. And he couldn't just light out to leave them floundering in the desert with Mangus Voya on the rampage. It was a quandary a man of Wink Jefford's disposition just couldn't ride around.

'The name's Abel Stoker,' the other man said, breaking the silence as he handed over a cigar. They both lit up. 'Perhaps a few draws on this will help settle your mind in our favour.'

Wink nodded his thanks. A few appreciative puffs worked wonders by focusing his thoughts. Taking on this job could certainly be compared with scouting for the army in many respects. The two men sat facing each other, the older one silently urging this intrepid stranger to grasp the nettle. And it was Wink who finally broke the impasse holding out a hand.

'They call me Wink Jefford,' he announced studying Stoker's face for any sign of abhorrence. The wagon master merely smiled innocently, accepting the positive gesture. Clearly the incident at Defiance had not reached Carrizozo by the time these folks left. 'One condition if'n I do take this on,' he posited. Stoker raised a questioning eyebrow. 'You look after these folks and leave me to do all the scouting. I ain't harbouring no desire to be a nursemaid.'

Stoker breathed a sigh of relief. 'Much obliged, Wink. It sure appears to have been our lucky day you happening along.'

'Don't count your blessing too soon, Abel,' he cautioned. 'This is rough country and we still have a week's travel ahead of us. A lot can happen in that time.' Little did he realize the prophetic nature of that remark.

Stoker frowned. 'They told me in Carrizozo that we could reach Tularosa in a week and that was four days since.'

'If'n you want to keep your hair, take my advice and go around by the Isadora Divide.' He pointed towards a break in the mountain chain in the opposite direction to their current line of travel. 'The trail is longer but at least there's a waterhole at Atoka Springs. More important though, it's a heap safer. The direct route is held by Mangus and his bunch. No way do you want to meet up with that guy.'

A resigned shrug of acceptance saw Abel Stoker agreeing to the detour. 'Guess you're the boss now when it comes to scouting matters.'

'That's what you're paying me for,' Wink agreed. 'Now, let's turn these wagons around. We still have a couple of hours left before sundown.'

'First off, I'll introduce you to the others and give them the low-down on what we've decided.' Stoker swung his horse round, heading back towards the first wagon. 'This is my wife Rachel and her sister Angie.' Wink tipped his hat to both women as Stoker explained the scout's purpose for joining the train. But the newcomer was not listening. His full attention was glued to the younger of the two females. The sun glinted off golden tresses affording a beatific image that had the scout mesmerized. For once he was lost for words.

'Are these Apaches as fierce as we've been told, Mister Jefford?' Angie Henstridge enquired, initially unaware of the startling effect she had produced in this handsome stranger. 'They say Indians are especially attracted to white girls.'

Her sister butted in immediately. 'Don't talk like that, Angela,' the starchy madam remonstrated fearfully. 'It makes me shudder to think what our fate would be if we fell into their hands.'

A coquettish chuckle from the delectable Miss Henstridge was aimed at the enthralled newcomer. 'I'm sure that our new scout will keep us safe from any harm.' Eyes large as saucers held Wink prisoner, although on this occasion he was more than happy to be shackled. 'Isn't that so, Mister Jefford?'

The interjection brought the enthralled captive back down to earth. 'D-don't you w-worry none, ma'am,' he assured them both with a stutter, trying desperately to swallow down his naïvety where woman were concerned. A brief moment to compose himself followed before he was able to shift the talk onto firmer ground. 'I'll make sure you don't come to any harm. We're taking the longer route to Tularosa. Hopefully that way we can avoid a confrontation.'

'It certainly looks like we're in safe hands,' Angie Henstridge remarked whimsically to her companion.

'Reckon we ought to get moving,' Stoker butted in, impatient to terminate the awkward chatter. 'This ain't the time to scaremonger, Angie,' he rebuked his sister-in-law sternly. 'We're in dangerous territory and can do without any frivolous remarks like that.' He turned his attention back towards the scout.

'Maybe you should ride ahead, Wink, and find us a good campsite for the night.'

The new scout once again tipped his hat to the two ladies, the ardent gaze of the younger one pursuing him until he disappeared from view. Rachel Stoker was quick to spot the emotive spark their new scout had aroused in her sister. 'That squint in his left eye is so endearing,' the younger woman mooned with a sigh. 'Gives him a rugged, fine-looking appeal. Don't you think so, Rachel?'

The sulky look and the puckered brow intimated that her sister was none too pleased. Indeed, she had the opposite view. 'I don't honestly know what you see in the man, Angela,' she scolded haughtily. 'It's indecent you thinking such unwholesome thoughts about a drifter you've only just met. Me and Abel were hoping you would marry his brother Frank when we reach Tularosa.'

The abrupt suggestion certainly had the desired effect of popping Angie's starry-eyed bubble, but not in the manner Rachel would have wished. 'I've never given you any sign that I'm interested in Frank,' she shot back tartly. 'Sure, he's OK, but I'll be the one to decide who I will or won't take for a husband.' A tense silence followed as Angie took up the leathers and slapped the team back into motion.

During the evening stopover, Wink was kept busy checking the wagons and becoming acquainted with the other members of the party. Some were like the Stokers, headed for land already purchased. Others just wanted a fresh start. Sitting round the campfire that night, the scout remained firmly tight-lipped regarding the unsavoury blemish on his exemplary record. It would only take one mistake, one careless remark to bring discredit down upon his head once again.

That said, he was equally set on protecting the train from any attack, should it occur. Talk inevitably shifted towards the Indian threat. Wink explained that much of southern New Mexico had been Mimbreno Apache land since time immemorial and they were violently adamant that it would remain so. All intruders were accordingly regarded as trespassers who needed eradicating. Accordingly, any form of compromise had failed dismally thus far.

Wink Jefford leaned more towards the peacemaking faction and quietly argued his case with those settlers who would have condemned him out of hand had they known of his recent trouble at Fort Defiance. It was an uphill struggle; he did not want to press too hard. After all, he was one of them and had been hired to lead these people to their avowed destination.

Guadalupe was one of the few Apache chiefs supportive of a truce that would satisfy all factions. Others of a less conciliatory nature such as the fiery Mangus Voya obdurately believed that only death of the invaders would appease the evil spirits. The conflict between followers of the diametrically opposing views spouted by Mangus and Colonel Dennison could only ever terminate in wholesale bloodshed.

By the time he had checked that the camp was

safely battened down for the night and sentries had been set, it was too late to pay a much sought after visit to the Stoker wagon. Next morning he and Angie were only able to exchange a brief smile, a quick salutation in passing as the train was readied for another day on the trail.

Around midday, the open terrain they were following was being funnelled steadily into what appeared to be an impassable barrier of blunt-edged tableland. The deep red sandstone was topped by a singular rock formation with the appropriate handle of Church Butte. 'How we gonna get through that?' Stoker exclaimed, a sweeping arm taking in the apparently impassable obstruction. The two men had been riding ahead of the train.

Wink showed no concern. 'To the right of Church Butte, there's a break in the canyon wall. It's narrow but no problem for wagons in single file. I'll ride up ahead and make sure it's safe.'

'Do you think there might be Indians waiting to ambush us?' Stoker's voice was edgy with nervousness. 'You said we'd be OK going this way.' The brittle tone held a note of accusation.

Wink shrugged. 'Nobody can predict what a critter like Mangus Voya will do. This is his land and he knows every inch like the back of his hand. It's always best to check first. You stay with the train. Keep them moving steadily towards the Church.'

A light slap on the rump and Patch leapt forward. Stoker's sceptical gaze followed him as he disappeared over the crest of a white dune before swinging his own horse around. The lines around his mouth tightened. Had he made the right decision in placing all his trust and the safety of his dependants in the hands of this unknown stranger?

A couple of miles further on, Wink slowed his horse to a walk. The lazy eye squinted at the tracks of unshod ponies heading into the canyon ahead. Straight away he knew that trouble was brewing. His caution had been well founded, and to prove the point, smoke signals on the heights above began passing messages between the rebels hidden in the rocky enclave through which the wagon train was due to pass. They must have spotted the scout below. It was now imperative that he return to the train and organize its defence against the imminent attack.

Heading back to the train, his eye caught sight of one set of tracks that were out of place. He paused leaning down to take a closer look. No mistake. His brow furrowed in puzzlement. A shod horse had made this set. Was it the same bushwhacker who had gunned down Shinto? It seemed highly likely; the coincidence was too great to ignore.

So what did it mean? There was no time to ponder on that conundrum now. Urgent action was needed to protect the settlers.

FIVE

TORN FLAG

The galloping appaloosa crested a rise some three miles north of Church Rock Canyon. From the dust cloud in his wake it was obvious that Jefford had urgent news to impart. Stoker brought the wagons to a halt as the scout dragged Patch to a thundering halt. He pointed back the way he had come. 'There's Indians up ahead. Get these wagons on the move,' he urged. 'We need a place to defend ourselves.'

Stoker's grim expression indicated his displeasure at the scout's decision to bring them this way. 'We should have stuck to the shortcut, then we could have reached Tularosa safely,' he berated the scout.

Wink's biting riposte chopped down any argument. 'I said that Mangus could be anywhere in these mountains. This is his land. You were mighty fortunate not to have been attacked before now. Get these wagons moving pronto! This ain't no time to bandy words. Those critters will be here soon.'

The brittle diktat brooked no wrangling as he rode up and down the line, waving his hat and urging the drivers to head for a sharp angle in the cliffs he had spotted a half mile ahead. Within minutes, the whole caboodle was galloping hell for leather towards place he had stipulated.

All the while, Wink kept an eye open for the Indians, who by this time would have grasped that their planned ambush had been sussed. 'Get the wagons in a semicircle with the horses and cattle inside,' he directed the men feverishly. 'Everybody, make sure your weapons are fully loaded.'

One of the settlers pulled Abel Stoker to one side. 'Do think this guy knows what he's doing?' he whispered nervously. 'We haven't seen any sign of Indians and now he's scaring us into believing we're under attack.'

The wagon master was equally nonplussed, but was ready to back the scout's assessment of the situation nonetheless. After all, it was he who had hired him, and he didn't want to give the impression his own judgement had been at fault. 'I figure he knows more about this land than any of us. Best we give him the chance to prove it.'

Nothing more was said as Wink hurried over, with the two women following behind. 'I'm going to hide these two up in the rocks. They'll be safer up there.'

'We don't need to hide away, Mister Jefford,' Rachel Stoker protested. 'I can shoot a rifle as good as any man. Ain't that so, Abel?'

Wink didn't give her husband chance to reply. 'Believe me, ma'am,' he insisted. 'You don't want to be taken by the Apaches if'n they do manage to overrun the encampment. Now do as I advise and follow me. Those bucks will be massing out there ready to attack.'

'Do as he says, Rachel,' Stoker said. 'Your'n and Angie's safety has to be my number one priority.'

The two woman tagged behind Wink reluctantly, up into the lower belt of broken rocks behind the redoubt. He soon found what he was looking for: a small cave that he indicated for the women to enter. 'Stay here and don't come out until this shindig is over.' He then uprooted a small mesquite bush and placed it over the entrance. 'You'll be safe in there.'

Those were his final words before dropping back down to check the makeshift fortification could withstand an attack. Wink then made sure all the men were spaced out at regular intervals around the half circle formed by the wagons. All eyes faced the direction from which the anticipated attack would come. An hour passed and still there was no sign of any movement outside the protective cordon.

'You sure those red devils are out there?' a sceptical Abel Stoker enquired. 'We ain't seen a single redskin since leaving Carrizozo.' Others in the party were likewise beginning to utter cynical comments regarding the scout's dependability. The sun had edged over the surrounding ramparts. Sinewy shadows were creeping across the sand like the searching tentacles of some primordial beast.

45

'They're out there. You can bet on that,' Wink asserted with conviction. 'Likely they won't attack before dawn now. But I want sentries posted throughout the night to make sure we ain't caught out. Two hours on, two off for each man.'

Soon after, darkness enfolded the camp in a tight grip that did nothing to ease the unsettling mood. Only with the lighting of cooking fires and the serving of hot food did the tension diminish somewhat. Wink insisted that the two women remain secluded, bedding and food being taken up to their hideout.

Conversation was desultory. All thoughts were focused on what the coming day might bring – death and destruction or relief and the continuation of their journey unsullied by the scout's outlandish claims. It was for the latter that all the settlers were silently praying. Wink Jefford, however, was under no illusions that an attack would materialize.

Night passed with little sleep for any of the settlers. It was with nervous expectation that the false dawn broke across the eastern skyline. A pale orange corona slowly blossomed into streaks of indigo purple and yellow. A mesmerising sight, were it not for the prediction alleged by their scout.

As the shadows began to disperse, Stoker challenged Wink's claim. 'Looks like you were wrong, fella,' he scoffed in a belittling tone. 'There ain't no Indians around, so we'll continue along the more direct route like what I'd planned in the first place. And you, mister, are fired.'

No sooner were the words out of his mouth than a gunshot echoed round the enclosed circlet of rocks. A scream followed as one of the men tumbled off his wagon, dead before his body hit the ground. Moments later, the swish of a fire arrow buried itself in the white canvas of the same wagon. Hungry flames gorged on the material as another found a second home. Panic gripped the defenders.

Only Wink kept a cool head, palming his six-shooter instantly and triggering off a couple of shots at the Apache who had loosed the arrows. The Indian pitched forward, landing just in front of the cave where the women were hidden before bouncing off and tumbling in a heap of flying limbs.

Before the body had even hit the ground inside the cordon, Wink was issuing orders. Only one man moved to obey, and then only to grab a bucket of water and toss the contents over the gobbling blaze. 'No water!' Wink shouted. 'Use sand to douse the flames. Out here we need every drop for ourselves.'

The others were just standing around mesmerized by the sudden change in their fortunes. He knew that rapid action was needed to get these greenhorns into action. Pushing and berating urgently, he organized them into some kind of order.

'You men, douse those fires,' he instructed. 'The rest of you get behind the wagons. And keep your heads down.'

And it was none too soon either. The whooping and hollering of bloodthirsty Apaches assailed their ears, sending shivers down their spines as it was so intended. A dozen or more Indians, all painted up for war, suddenly appeared and hammered across the open sward. Shots rang out immediately as the defenders triggered their rifles nervously. 'Don't open fire until they come within range,' the scout directed steadfastly. 'Wait until I give the order, then make every shot count.'

Wink peered along the line. Some men had gritted their teeth, their cheeks sighting along old Spencer rifles. Others were literally shaking with fear. 'Hold your nerve, boys,' he encouraged. 'With God on our side, we'll win the day. Ready. . . .' His order hung in the air as the Indians rattled closer. They were almost on top of the defenders when the order came. 'Fire!'

Two of the attackers were hit by the fusillade immediately. The others swerved to one side, some loosing off arrows, others firing rifles. Another defender went down with an arrow in his chest. One doughty brave veered towards a gap in the wagons, flinging himself off his horse onto the back of another settler. The man stood no chance as the howling buck raised his knife, ready to drive it down into the exposed torso. A more terrifying sight for simple pioneers could not be imagined.

Quick to react, Wink pumped a couple of shots into the assailant, saving his victim's life. He hurried across, dragging the dead Indian off the cowering settler. 'On your feet, mister,' he rapped out, pushing the stunned man's gun back into his hands. 'Now get back in line.' This was no time for dithering.

Three times the raiding party made darting skirmishes at the wagons, twisting their ponies to present difficult targets to hit. Another wagon had caught a fire arrow, removing men from the barricade to extinguish the flames.

Following their final attack the raiders turned tail, retreating to the safety of the buttress, behind which the main band was hidden. The initial sally had done its job of demoralization, unnerving the defenders effectively. Mangus Voya watched from a high vantage point. A grim smile of hate warped the gnarled features. He had lost three men, but that was acceptable to the Mimbreno chieftain.

Now he would carry out the second part of his plan, which was to let the white dogs sweat, not knowing when or if their foe would strike again. The waiting game was a ploy that Indians often used to unsettle their victims. Time was on his side. And the longer he held back, the more they would begin to assume their aggressors had taken fright and disappeared. Their guard would be down. That was the moment to strike.

Wink was well versed in such tactics. So when the dazed and penitent wagon-master approached him some time later, he was ready with an answer to the expected question. 'Do you figure we've scared them off?' Stoker asked hopefully, not deigning to mention his previously belligerent attitude. 'We ain't seen hide nor hair of them since that last attack.'

All of Stoker's efforts following the first attack had been to douse the fires. Unfortunately two of the

49

wagons had been totally destroyed. All that remained were smoke-blackened hulks. The owners could only stand and stare open-mouthed as all their worldly possessions smouldered in the ashes. Despair was evident in their hollow-eyed stares.

Wink was sympathetic, but at least they were still drawing breath, unlike the three that had perished in the assault. 'They ain't finished yet,' he posited firmly. 'Not by a long chalk. Mangus expects you to think he's given up and slunk away. We need to be extra vigilant, now more than ever, to survive.'

He was loath to express his true feelings. These men were not soldiers well versed in warfare against Indians. As such, they had failed to heed his advice and had expended most of their ammunition. Even the guns they possessed were old models such as the Springfield and Ballard single shot breechloaders. Another attack by the main body with Mangus at their head would surely finish them off.

Wink gritted his teeth. There was only one course of action open to him.

'I'm going out there to parley with him.' He tore off a piece of white canvas from one of the wagons and tied it to broom handle. 'I'll plead your case and hope that he shows us some mercy.'

Stoker was not convinced. 'What makes you think that murderous skunk will listen to you?'

'I did him a service once.' He didn't elaborate. The Fort Defiance incident was unlikely to be well received. 'And I'm figuring it will persuade him to look on my petition with favour.'

'You sure that's wise?' muttered the sceptical wagon master. 'He could kill you and leave us wide open to another attack.'

'Unless you can think of better suggestion, it's the only way.' A blank look of despondency saw the scout spurring off, the white flag of appeasement clearly in evidence. He was met by two bucks who had been told to watch the camp. He drew up when they barred his path, raising a hand to show he meant them no harm. 'Take me to your leader. I have words only for his ears.'

Silently, the braves escorted Wink to where their chief had made camp. Blindfolded, the sentinels led him deep into the heart of the mountain fastness. The journey took about half an hour. Mangus was crouched in front of a quickly erected wickiup and smoking a pipe. He stood up as the returning guardians approached. The prisoner blinked when the blindfold was removed. A dozen or more of the low reed dwellings were ranged around a central fire on which a large pot was bubbling. It was a temporary camp, easily dismantled when the need arose.

Seeing the white flag the chief was fully mindful of the scout's mission. 'You are brave, white man, to venture into our camp alone. But foolish if you think Mimbreno warriors are any less strong than our Chirucahua cousins. None of the Apache will show mercy to the invaders of our land.'

'I come only to seek peace with the Apache,' the messenger replied. Mangus threw out a mocking grunt. Wink realized that he had an uphill struggle on his hands. Yet all he could do now was persist and trust that common sense would shine through. 'It was I who saved your son from a firing squad. Ask Shinto and he will agree that I am a true friend. Most of my people want to live in harmony with their red brothers. Mangus must see that there is enough room in this land for us all.'

The snarl issuing from the throat of Mangus Voya sounded like an angry lion. He stepped forward, brandishing his rifle. Wink's eyes were drawn to the new Winchester. How in blue blazes had he gotten hold of that? He was not given the chance to ponder the enigma.

'You speak to me of sharing Apache birthright,' he growled out. 'That will never come to pass. My son has no white friends. Every last one of your kind is enemy of the Apache. Your mission for mercy has been wasted. No weakness can be shown while the hated invaders steal our homeland.' He nodded to a brave standing behind the scout.

A rifle butt slammed into Wink's head. The last he recalled was tumbling headlong down into a deep pit of blackness. When he finally came to, the sun was high in the sky and beating down on his exposed body with unrestrained fury. He tried to rise, but movement was severely limited. With fear gripping his innards, he quickly grasped the enormity of his position.

SIX

STAKEOUT . . .

Tethered to the ground, he was staked out like a sheet of drying cowhide somewhere beyond the camp. Much as he strove to free his trapped limbs, the feeble thrashing only served to bind him tighter. A sweat-coated face turned away from the blistering heat that was slowly burning him up, but there was no escape.

Never before had Wink Jefford found himself in such desperate straits. Was this how it was going to end? Shrivelled up like an old boot having failed miserably to protect the wagon train. There was not even enough moisture left in his body for tears of despair.

His eyes closed, yet still the glaring orb showed him no compassion. Then, all of a sudden, darkness fell. Was it night already and he had just woken up? His eyes opened slowly to reveal a figure leaning over him, blocking out the sun. Hope flared of a rescue but was dashed instantly when he saw the knife, its blade glinting in the harsh light. So this was to be his end. At least he would not suffer the agonies of being burnt alive by the sun.

Breathing hard, he waited for the lethal slash to end it all. Then a low voice permeated his addled brain. 'Was it you, white man, who rescued my son from the bluecoats, then again when he had been shot?' Wink struggled to focus his vision. Overhead, buzzards were circling in feverish anticipation. But it was the voice that registered inside his scorched brain, a woman's voice.

The hazy features of a squaw swam into view. Distinctly noticeable was the cerebral grace shining through the ribbed façade that could have been hewn from a slab of orange sandstone. This woman had presence, and it was clear she was no bond-servant.

His lips moved, but nothing emerged. The tongue in his mouth felt like a lump of dried leather. All he could do in answer to the query was nod. Then the knife went to work, slitting the strands of leather binding his limbs. 'Go quickly before my husband returns,' she urged, dribbling water between his dry lips. It felt like the nectar of the gods. 'There is a horse for you. Go by way of mountain pass.' She pointed to a notch on the horizon. 'That way you will avoid Mangus and the others when they return.'

She helped him up, pushing the goatskin water gourd into his hands. 'Not all Indians are bitter and filled with hate like Mangus. I, Nalin, mother of Shinto, share the desire for peace, to settle in one place and cease this endless wandering.'

'You don't have the look of an Apache,' Wink said, stretching to ease the stiffness from tight muscles.

I am Yaqui,' Nalin replied, helping Wink to his feet. 'Mangus kept me for his woman. My people were captured. Most were sold into slavery.' Age and the ravages of repression had scoured out hollows and grooves but had dismally failed to destroy a once beautiful woman. Long black hair tied back in a plait was secured by a red headband, redolent of the Apache style of dress. A dark look of anguish rolled across the woman's leathery features. 'The only good to come from it was my son.'

The wistful longing for times past dissolved quickly as pragmatism reasserted itself. 'Quickly, you must go,' she stressed, helping him rise. Eyes black as ebony darted hither and thither, fearful that her betrayal would be exposed.

Wink needed no second bidding. He thanked the woman. 'I will not forget Nalin's courage in her actions this day.' And with that, he urged the unshod Indian pony up the steep slope. When he looked around, the sympathetic woman had disappeared. Wink shuddered to think what her fate would be should the disloyalty come to light.

It was three days later that he finally stumbled out of the mountains and down to join the main trail south, and there he abandoned the pony with its woven blanket. These animals possessed a homing instinct that would lead it back to the Mimbrano camp. Riding an unshod Indian pony would not be a wise move in the current outbreak of hostilities. There would be too many tricky questions to answer, and by then he hoped to be well clear of the Sacramento Mountains.

Wink sat down on a rock beside the well-used trail. It was another hour before he spotted the telltale sign of an approaching column of freight wagons. The leading muleskinner hauled rein. 'Guess you must be wanting a ride, fella,' a grizzled pioneer commented, obvious puzzlement clouding his weathered visage. 'Mighty strange place to meet someone, out here in the wilds.'

Wink had a ready answer to hand. 'My horse was bitten by a rattler up in the hills. I've been on foot for the last two days. Lucky for me you came along.'

The old guy accepted the reason without blinking. He shifted across the bench seat, allowing Wink to climb up beside him. 'We're five days out of Albuquerque headed for Tularosa if'n that suits you.'

'Much obliged.' Wink was genuinely grateful. 'That's where I'm heading as well. How long do you figure it will take us?'

'We'll stop off for the night at Blackwall Springs. All being well we should be hauling into Tularosa day after tomorrow.' The man held out a hand. 'Cracker Jack Torrance. I'm the chief teamster of this shebang.'

Wink accepted the gesture, keeping a sharp watch on the fella's reaction when he introduced himself.

56

'My name's Wink Jefford.' There was nary a flicker of hesitation in the old timer's expression as he lived up to his nickname with a spirited *yip yip*. The huge bull-whip snaked out, tickling the right ear of the lead mule as the train lumbered back into motion. Watching the skill with which the old guy handled that whip captivated the passenger. A deft flick and he could have made those mules dance a jig.

Cracker Jack was a talkative guy. When he wasn't going on colourfully about the fortunes he had made and lost while prospecting, it was the current Indian problem that was on his mind.

'That Mangus Voya is one mean critter. Only yesterday he ambushed a patrol out of Fort Defiance,' he espoused, not noticing his associate's whole body stiffen up. 'More'n half of those soldier boys were chopped down afore you could say boo to a goose. The others somehow managed to escape with their hair intact. All apart that is from the officer in command. I heard all the grizzly details from a trapper when we stopped at Pegleg Nelson's Trading Post.'

No mention was made of the wagon train, which led Wink to surmise that Abel Stoker had managed to hold them off. He didn't feel it prudent to mention his own association with the settlers. Torrance fell silent while he wrestled the team of eight down a rough slope.

Only when they were on level ground once again did he add the mind-bending corollary of the story. 'It appears that Mangus has a beef against Defiance's commanding officer for capturing his son and threatening him with a firing squad. And he would have, too, if'n some jasper hadn't helped him to escape.' Wink almost fell out of his seat. If this fella only knew whom he was sitting next to, his passenger might well find himself cast adrift. Unheeding, Torrance merely continued with the story, ignorant of his passenger's involvement. 'Bunk Adderley, the trapper, reckons he's gonna send the officer's head back to the fort to show he means business. Real nice kinda guy, ain't he?'

Wink swallowed down his anxiety before remarking, 'I've come across Colonel Dennison before.' He coughed to hide the edgy huskiness in his throat. 'And I know for sure that he'll never send out a rescue party just to save one officer.'

Cracker Jack was having none of that. He scoffed at the notion. 'He might change his mind when he learns that the hostage they're holding is his only son.'

The blood drained from Wink's face. This time his discomfiture was evident to the teamster. 'Looks like you've seen a ghost, boy,' was the searching observation.

'That could turn into a nasty situation,' Wink countered to allay any suspicion. 'I sure wouldn't want to be in Dennison's shoes. I wonder how he'll play it.'

Cracker responded with an unknowing shrug. 'Guess you're right there. For a jasper that hates Indians like what he does, it's a poser all right and no mistake. My betting is that Mangus will be counting on that to lay an ambush.'

Following a desultory silence as the two men mulled over the import of the revelations, Wink steered the conversation onto more mundane topics. Torrance was happy to oblige by relating how he had started up in the freighting business. Wink was listening with only half an ear. His thoughts were chewing over the dire predicament faced by Dennison senior.

And so the journey to Tularosa continued with, thankfully, no sign of the Apaches. As promised by the hauler, the mule train arrived at its destination just as the church clock was tolling the noon hour. Wink stepped down. 'Thanks again for the ride, Jack. I owe you one.'

'A drink will suit me fine, young fella. You'll find me propping up the bar in the Elkhorn saloon over yonder when I've finished unloading.' He raised the whip, ready to continue to the far end of town, before adding, 'And if'n you're ever in need of a job, I can always use another teamster.'

Wink nodded his thanks then headed the other way. He was anxious to find out if the wagon train had reached Tularosa. His answer came sooner than expected. Standing on the far side of the street was none other than Angie Henstridge and her sister. They were accompanied by a stranger. Wink assumed immediately this must be Abel Stoker's brother, but of Stoker himself there was no sign.

None of them looked pleased to see him. Angie

could not even bear to look him in the face. What was this all about? They had clearly managed to keep the Apache raiders at bay. With his thoughts churning over the fractious mood being aimed his way, he made to cross the busy street, only just avoiding a collision with a horse-drawn wagon. 'Sorry about that, mister,' he blurted out quickly stepping back.

'Don't speak to me, Judas,' the driver lambasted him. 'We don't want your kind in Tularosa.'

'What in thunder are you talking about?' exclaimed the mesmerized scout, lost for words. But the wagon had trundled on its way.

Having stumbled across to face the ugly deputation that had grown quickly, Wink was given no opportunity to question the reasoning behind this hostile reception. Frank Stoker stepped forward to confront him. 'I don't know how you have the gall to come here, Jefford, after what you've done,' he snarled, placing a protective arm around the shoulders of Angie Henstridge. 'Only a coward would abandon his duty to protect the wagon train and let those savages wipe everybody out to the last man. These two ladies were the only ones lucky enough to escape unscathed, no darned thanks to you.'

Grumbles of accord greeted this denunciation. Only Angie appeared uncomfortable. But her low-voiced disavowal of this accusation was ignored. The crowd was shuffling about, an atmosphere of menace threatening to bubble up. This patently had nothing to do with his actions at Fort Defiance. It was now obvious to Wink that Mangus had carried out his attack on the wagon train with ruthless precision. The women had been missed due to their concealment in the cave. How had they managed to reach safety? And why had neither spoken up on his behalf?

The first query was answered by Stoker. 'The sheriff organized a rescue mission when they didn't show up on time. Burying those mutilated bodies is the worst thing I've ever had to do.'

Again, growls of anger rumbled through the gathering crowd. Wink knew he was in deep trouble unless he acted quickly to squash the wholesale belief that he had wilfully forsaken the settlers leaving them to a grim fate. Knowing his own life hung in the balance, he avidly proceeded to declare his innocence. 'It's not true that I abandoned the train. Didn't I hide you two ladies inside that cave?' A beseeching regard pleaded with the survivors to back his claim.

Angie remained silent, merely nodding, while her sister agreed this was the case. She then proceeded to deliver the killing blow. 'All I saw after the first attack was this man riding off with two Indians. It looked to me like he knew them and was leaving us to our fate.' Tears of anguish bubbled over as she added, 'My husband was the last one to die. And it was all his fault.'

'That ain't true,' shouted Wink angrily. 'I was after persuading Mangus to show mercy because of help I'd given to his son.'

'Hear that, boys?' Stoker railed. 'The yellow skunk

61

has been condemned by his own words. He's an Indian-lover. And he's come here figuring nobody would have survived the massacre to denounce him. What we gonna do about it?'

'Hang the bastard!' called out one irate watcher.

'Ain't no need for a trial,' agreed another. 'We all know he's guilty as sin.'

Odious roars of approval hailed these verdicts. Someone threw a noose over a tree branch. The crowd began to close in. Like the tentacles of some gigantic octopus, arms reached forward to secure their prey. The die was cast. Before Wink had time to react, his gun was removed from its holster and his arms were pinioned.

Through the misty haze, he could see that Frank Stoker had stepped back, a sinister smile warping the handsome features. He had clearly spread the judgmental word around Tularosa, including a description of the accused man should he appear. The guy's mystifying work of undermining the scout had succeeded. Now others could finish the job.

But what was his game? Was it jealousy when he had learned from Rachel Stoker of Angie's attraction to him? Or was there some other unknown reasoning behind the devious ploy? With his brother dead, the land would be passed on to him, like as not. But how did that affect Wink Jefford?

He was given no chance to mull over these conundrums as the unruly crowd pushed him towards the hanging tree. At that moment, Angie finally found her voice, crying out. 'You can't do this. He did try to save us.' But her plea was drowned out by the incensed bloodlust of the mob.

Help was at hand when the blast from a shotgun brought the stumbling throng to a halt. County sheriff Troy Vickery jumped up onto the boardwalk, the gun cradled in his arms. A deputy joined him. Both men eyed the milling crowd. 'There'll be no vigilante law in Tularosa while I'm in charge,' Vickery declared, taunting the agitated mob to ignore the recharged twin barrels of the Loomis scattergun. He gestured to the deputy. 'Bring him up here, Cab.'

'I never took you for a guy who would back a lily-livered coward like him,' Frank Stoker challenged the lawman. 'A rat like that don't deserve protection from the law. Ain't that so, boys?' Angry shouts of agreement threatened to overwhelm the two star packers.

But Troy Vickery was no milksop. He stood his ground fearlessly. 'If'n any man here can accuse me of backing wilful murder, let him speak up now.' He looked around, searching out any dissenters. Nobody spoke up. 'OK then. Until a law is passed by the territorial legislature stating that cowardice is a crime, I'll not allow judgement by mob rule to hold sway. Lock him up!'

The deputy elbowed aside the shuffling mob to escort the prisoner across to the jailhouse. 'Any man that tries to take the law into his own hands will receive a load of buckshot,' Vickery warned. 'And I can assure you all that such action is backed up in the law books. Now break this up and go about your business.'

Still the mob hesitated. Stoker had done a good job in firing them up. A shot from Cab Smollett's pistol into the ground at their feet punched home the blunt message that the lawmen were not intimidated, nor would they be cowed by threats. Stoker gritted his teeth but remained silent. Sooner or later the sheriff would have to release Wink Jefford. That was when he would arrange for his removal.

He led the two women away. Only Angie Henstridge appeared concerned for the accused man's welfare. Stoker was too wrapped up in his own plans for the inherited land section to notice the concern etched across the girl's anxious façade. 'Don't bother your head about that critter,' he remarked blithely. 'When we're married, everything will be fine. And there'll always be a home for you as well, Rachel. Just because my brother's land has been passed down to me don't make you any less a part of this family.'

'That's very thoughtful of Frank, isn't it Angie?' she said. But her younger sister was not listening. She covered up her hesitancy by walking on ahead.

SEVEN

. . . AND BREAK OUT!

Inside the jailhouse, Wink was trying desperately to convince the marshal that he was totally innocent of the charge of cowardice. He explained what had happened when he reached the Indian encampment.

But the lawman was unbending. 'Those were good people. The Stokers are well liked around here. Abel had gone to Carrizozo to marry a new bride he'd met through a marriage bureau. And now he's dead. Rachel didn't deserve that. None of them deserved to die out there.' Vickery bunched his fists. He was good and mad.

'Don't you think I regret it as well?' Wink countered vehemently. But the plea for understanding washed over the guy's head.

'You were responsible for their safe passage and

you failed in your duty. There ain't no getting around that.' The tin star pushed the alleged prisoner roughly towards the open door of the lone cell. 'I'm holding you in here until that mob simmers down. Then I'll get you out of town. I fully sympathize with their anger. But the law is the law. And I'll uphold it with my life if'n needs be. Even for a yellow dog like you.'

An hour later, Vickery left the jail, ordering his deputy to keep the door locked. 'I'm going over to the Elkhorn to make sure those jaspers have quieted down.' Opening the door he was surprised to find Angie Henstridge outside. 'Could I speak with the prisoner, Sheriff?' she asked anxiously. 'I need to hear his version.'

Vickery was reluctant but acquiesced on seeing her earnest manner. 'Don't be long, miss. A jail ain't no place for a woman.' And with that he departed, leaving Angie nervous as she approached the locked cell. The incarcerated man didn't look up as she made a plea to hear his side of the grim event.

No response was forthcoming so she tried again. 'I want to believe in you, Wink,' the woman insisted tentatively. 'But the others were so convinced you had deserted them, I couldn't be sure in my own mind.'

This time he turned to face her. 'If'n you felt that way, you should have spoken up out there.' Wink's reply was brusque, a wounding bite. 'Seems to me that you still ain't sure.'

'I tried to speak out. But they wouldn't listen.'

66

Wink was not won over. 'Well, you didn't try hard enough. It's too late now.'

He turned aside. There was no way he was going to plead for understanding. 'I reckon it will be best all round if'n you do what's expected and marry that guy.'

An impasse a mile wide had opened up between them. With no more to be said, a distraught Angie Henstridge left the jail. Deputy Smollett locked the door behind her, unaware that a pair of watchful eyes was keeping him under close scrutiny through a sky-light opening onto the roof of the single storey jail. Lying flat to avoid being spotted by anybody in the street below, Shinto was patiently awaiting an oppor-tunity to upset the applecart.

The young Indian had followed his saviour to Tularosa, having been persuaded that the white man was indeed a friend to the Apache cause. The furore he had covertly encountered against the scout left him in no doubt that Wink Jefford's life was in mortal danger. Only one course of action could be taken to prevent mob rule holding sway. A rescue would have to be mounted and a debt repaid.

So here he was, opening the window carefully, a knife stuck between his teeth. The resolute determi-nation not to be swayed from his lethal endeavour was akin to that of a lion stalking its prey.

The first that either man knew of the alien pres-ence was when Shinto dropped silently onto the deputy's back as he was walking across to the stove for a cup of coffee. Smollett was taken completely by surprise. No cry of alarm issued from his mouth, such was the rapidity of the attack. His assailant wasted no time in removing any threat the deputy might have posed. Before Wink could express any opposition to such a deadly outcome, the blade had been buried in the exposed back.

Smollett had stood no chance. The deputy's body lay splayed across the wooden floor, blood pumping from the fatal wound. Shinto's stony regard showed no remorse as he grabbed the cell key to release his friend. The freed man was less than enthusiastic with Shinto's interference. Vickery had promised to get him out of town.

That opportunity had now been shot to ribbons. 'Why in thunder did you have to kill him?' Wink protested. 'The law was on my side. I could have been out of here tomorrow. Now they're bound to assume I killed him.'

'I had to do this for you,' Shinto insisted as Wink retrieved his gun belt. 'The leader of this pack of wolves is out there now pushing them to hang you. With the sheriff out of the way they will have a free hand. You cannot find the white man who told my father about the wagon train while hanging from a tree. Come quick,' he urged, pushing the liberated scout towards the back door. 'Soon much fire water will give mob the courage to march on jail.'

'Are you saying that a white man set those poor folks up?' Wink was dumbfounded by the allegation. 'Who was it?'

'I do not know. Only my father can tell you. Now we go.'

A rapping on the front door alerted Wink to the dire predicament he was in. 'Come on, hurry up and open this door, Cab. We need to shift Jefford to a safer place.' A second bout of knocking followed, this time louder and more urgent. 'What in thunder you doing in there?'

A side door opened onto an alleyway. The two escapees hustled out. 'I have horse round back. We will have to ride double.' Already an angry crowd was gathering. One of them spotted the absconders. 'Hey, look, boys!' he yelled out. 'Some redskin has released Jefford.' Immediately, guns were drawn. A fusillade of shots pursued the fugitives. Luckily, too much whiskey had soured their aim. Angry screams of hot lead nevertheless chased them round the back corner of the jail chewing slivers of wood from the frame.

Wink paused to draw his own revolver. A quick look round the edge, then he let rip to deter any pursuit, ensuring his aim was deliberately high. The last thing he needed was a real killing on his hands. Panic gripped the mob as they sought shelter desperately, giving the fugitives chance to dash over to where Shinto had tethered a stolen horse that was ready saddled. Wink leapt onto its back with Shinto clinging on behind. He dug his heels into the flanks, urging the animal forward. But the reprieve enabling the fugitives to make good their flight was only temporary.

The cry had gone up that the prisoner had killed Deputy Smollett. All hell broke loose immediately.

Frank Stoker was in the thick of the mêlée urging them on. 'Don't let the killer get away, men. The law is on our side now.'

That was the moment Lady Luck saw fit to surrender her indulgence. Shinto cried out as a bullet struck him in the back. Wink kept going until they were out of sight. He was forced to haul rein when the Indian tumbled off the back of the horse. The runaway tried to help him up, but Shinto knew his end was close.

'I am finished, white man,' he groaned. 'Go quickly before they come.' He then ripped a strikingly ornate spangler of silver and turquoise from around his neck and handed it to Wink. 'Take this to my father. It will ensure my spirit reaches the afterlife. The main camp is a day's ride beyond Atoka Springs.' The words tailed off as he gasped for air. 'Tell him I died bravely.'

The necklace glittered in the last rays of a dying sun. It was indeed a fine piece of Apache craftwork. His gaze shifted to the Indian for confirmation, but Shinto's eyes had glazed over. His head lolled to one side having breathed his last.

It struck Wink with a vengeance that had the Indian reached his horse first then he would be lying there instead of Shinto. The young brave had unwittingly saved his life, repaying a dept, albeit with the most conclusive of sacrifices. Wink owed him the respect of making good his escape. The noise of pursuit was already drawing close. Any minute now and they would be upon him. And with the obvious assumption that he was responsible for Cab Smollett's death, he would be lucky not to join the dead Indian in a pool of blood.

Reluctantly, he was forced to abandon Shinto and make good his getaway. It was greatly to his advantage that daylight was fading rapidly. The blurred approach of twilight cast a dark shadow, not merely over the material landscape but also the termination of a day that surely could not have ended any worse. He leapt onto the back of the horse with a fleeting ray of hope that at least he was still alive.

But for how long? He kicked the pony into motion and disappeared before the mob could vent their unrestrained fury.

When darkness made progress over the rough terrain more hazardous, he pulled off the trail into a shallow draw, and that was when he discovered that the Indian pony had been creased by a bullet and was leaking blood. He managed to stem the flow with the riding blanket. But it could only be a matter of time before the animal would have to be abandoned.

Next morning he was cheered by the fact that no further blood had been lost. Less than an hour on the trail, however, saw the horse faltering badly. With a heavy heart, Wink knew the end was nigh. He would have to put the poor beast out of its misery. The only way was with a sharp jab of his knife into the side of its head to pierce the brain. He could not afford a bullet; it might be heard by the posse he was certain would be hot on his heels. Death was instantaneous.

So now he was cast afoot and toting a heavy saddle. Not a situation to relish. All he could hope for was a miracle to deliver him from certain capture. And so it came to pass.

An hour later, with the sun beating down, Wink stumbled to the top of yet another sandy ridge. This one opened out into a broad valley where cattle could be seen grazing contentedly. Below him and close at hand was a fenced corral containing a dozen horses. A mile distant on the far side of valley bottom he could see the main ranch buildings. Smoke was rising from a chimney. Of human occupation in the immediate vicinity, however, there was no sign. Wink knew what he had to do.

He waited just below the crest of the hill to make certain the wrangler was otherwise engaged before dropping down the shallow grade. On approaching the corral he noticed one horse detach itself from the main group and trot over to the fence. Wink's eyes widened in disbelief. 'What in blue blazes are you doing here, Patch?' he exclaimed aloud, such was his shock. The appaloosa stallion had clearly recognized his old master from afar.

Wink badly needed a fresh horse and here was his own cayuse ready and waiting. But how had Patch found his way here, inside this corral? It was a puzzle to which the answer was irrelevant for the time being. He unfastened the gate. The faithful appaloosa snickered, nuzzling his master. 'It's good to see you too, old fella,' the scout cooed in the stallion's ear, stroking his mane with warm affection. 'All we need

72

to do now is get you saddled up.'

'Leave that saddle where it is, mister, and raise your hands.' The blunt order had come from a grizzled cowpoke who had appeared suddenly out of the blue. 'I spotted you up on that ridge and figured you were up to no good. Seems I was right. There ain't much worse than a horse thief.'

'But this is my horse,' protested Wink. 'I lost him after being caught by Mangus Voya and his bunch.' A true enough assertion, even though he was about to steal a horse from the corral anyway; for that, he had been caught bang to rights.

'This horse was bought by the boss in Tularosa,' the wrangler asserted, undaunted. 'I was with him when he signed the bill of sale. We have a mighty fine tree out back of the ranch for skunks like you. Now shift your ass, pronto.' The man gestured with his revolver, forcing Wink to do as bidden.

On questioning the wrangler it turned out that Wink had found himself traversing Running W land owned by a rancher called Corby Wishart. It abutted the Stoker holding. Further insistence from the alleged thief that the horse was his received a blunt response in the form of a hard jab from the wrangler's pistol. 'We'll let the boss decide that. And I can tell you, mister, he ain't too fond of horse thieves.'

Wishart was replacing some frayed saddle tack when the wrangler pushed the prisoner into the barn. An older man sporting a grey moustache, he eyed the newcomer with undisguised disdain from beneath thick-beetled brows. He and his wife had been in Tularosa at the time Wink had been accosted. 'You're the guy they were after hanging yesterday before Sheriff Vickery stepped in.' It was a brusque statement of fact with no indication of any welcome. 'So what's he doing on Running W land, Fletch?' he enquired of the wrangler.

'Caught him trying to steal that new appaloosa you bought from the livery man in Tularosa, boss.' Fletcher Boone hawked out a brittle laugh. 'The varmint even had the gall to claim it was his'n.'

'That so?' rasped Wishart. 'Around here we hang guys like you.'

Here was a man who had wrestled with the unforgiving landscape of southern New Mexico and come out the winner; someone who abhorred any kind of fickle chicanery that would be dealt with in a ruthless and decisive manner. Wishart was a man in stark contrast to the shifty-eyed Frank Stoker, who had inherited his land by reason of the tragic events that had led to Wink's current predicament.

The captive's rapid assessment adjudged this guy to be solidly reliable, the salt of the earth, and a man who supported justice and fair play. Nevertheless, Wink was fully aware that he would need all his acumen to convince Wishart he was telling the truth. He stood his ground, displaying no subservience to the danger he was in.

Indeed the rancher's threat made him all the more belligerent. He took a step forward. 'I'm getting a mite tired of folks accusing me of things I ain't done then threatening to string me up.'

74

Before he could express his anger in a more physical way, Boone stepped forward and slammed the barrel of his pistol across Wink's head. He went down grovelling on the floor. Blood was dribbling from a cut when Boone hauled him back onto his feet. 'Shall I get a rope, boss?' asked Idaho Newman, the other cowhand, who had been helping with the saddle repairs.

Corby Wishart studied the alleged culprit before speaking. 'I never did cotton to vigilante law. A man deserves a hearing at least before judgement is passed. So what's your story, fella? And make it good and short; I'm a busy man.'

Wink quickly outlined the events that had led to his current bleak prospects. It was only when he came to the escape and the knifing of Cab Smollett that Wishart interrupted. 'You darned fool. Now they can hang you legally.'

'But I never did it,' was the vehement rebuttal.

'That don't matter a jot where the law's concerned. You've shot your bolt good and proper, mister. But that's their business. My beef is that you were after stealing a horse. And round here, there's only one answer to that.'

'Patch must have somehow found a way through the mountains to end up here. That's his name. Let me call him over and you'll see that I'm telling the truth.' The rancher gave a desultory nod. 'Patch!' Wink called out. 'Over here, boy!' Dutifully, the loyal appaloosa trotted over, a rough tongue licking his master's face. 'See?' he pressed, tweaking the animal's ears. 'Don't that prove something? All I want now is to go find Mangus so he can clear my name.'

Wishart scratched his head. He was undecided. He had paid good money for that horse. 'Looks like you could be right, but that don't excuse you trying to steal him.' His manner towards the scout had, however, moderated somewhat. The story he told was convincing. He was particularly disturbed by the accusation that a white man had told the Indian raiders about the wagon train. But could he believe the word of a man everyone else was convinced was a coward, and a killer?

At that moment his wife Jolene appeared, calling him to the midday meal. When she saw the blood-stained figure being berated by her husband, the kindly soul hurried across. 'What's been going on here?' she said tartly, pushing them away. 'This man is hurt. That cut needs attention.'

The rancher's usual tough persona had returned. It did not do to display weakness in front of his men. 'We caught him trying to steal a horse. You know the penalty for that. And he's also broke jail.'

A strong-willed woman, Jolene Wishart ignored the bluster, leading the injured man over to the water trough to clean and dress the wound. Unsure what to do next, the men shuffled their feet. A shout from Fletcher Boone drew everyone's attention to the arrival of a group of riders whose dust had been spotted cresting a ridge midway along the valley. 'Looks like we've gotten more company,' he declared.

'That must be the posse,' Wink croaked out. 'They're after me.'

'We can let them handle things now,' Wishart declared, relieved that the responsibility would be taken out of his hands.

But his wife was having none of that. She pulled her husband aside. 'We don't know if this man is responsible for abandoning those settlers. He might well be telling the truth. You seem to have forgotten the time when you were in a similar position and needed help from a sympathetic friend.'

'I don't know, honey,' he prevaricated. 'It might all be a lie to gain our sympathy.' But Wishart's forlorn expression told her that his thoughts were harking back to the incident in question.

'Don't he deserve the same help, Corby?'

The posse was closing on the ranch rapidly. Another few minutes and they would arrive, and that would be that. A decision had to be made quickly. 'OK, hide him in the hay store. I'll stall them.' He then walked outside to greet the posse while his wife helped the fugitive into a place of sanctuary.

EIGHT

HI HO SILVER LINING!

The posse arrived moments later to be met outside the barn by Corby Wishart. 'You boys sure look in a hurry,' he declared, swallowing down his nervous trepidation. 'How can I help you?'

Sheriff Vickery peered around the cluster of buildings before replying. 'That darned jasper I was holding for his own safety has busted out of jail and killed my deputy.' The words emerged as a harsh staccato burst. 'We found his dead horse a-ways back and his prints led this way, but we lost the trail over by Rodwell Flatts.' He removed his hat, wiping the sweat from his brow. 'You spotted any suspicious characters hanging around, Corby? He's gonna need a horse to leave the territory.'

The sheriff skewered the rancher with a probing

look, aimed at digging through any flummery. He was by nature a sceptical jigger; it came with the job. Wishart considered the question before looking his wrangler in the eye. 'I haven't seen no stranger around here. How about you, Fletch?'

Boone and he had been together a long time. A bond existed between them that few issues could break. 'Nary a thing, boss,' he replied with not the tiniest flicker of hesitation. 'Reckon this guy must have headed the other way into the mountains. But we'll sure keep a look out for him.'

The sheriff accepted the negative response unreservedly. 'Don't matter none,' he shrugged. 'We'll soon pick up his trail. Jackdaw here is a first rate tracker. It's only a matter of time before we run the skunk to ground. OK, boys, mount up and let's be going.'

Jolene Wishart considered herself to be an excellent judge of character. The scout in her view was telling the truth. Consequently, stalling tactics were needed to help him make good his escape. She quickly stepped forward. 'You fellas look a mite tuckered out after all this tracking. A tired man makes mistakes. You could easily follow a dead trail without some rest. And I've just made a meal. There's enough for us all in the house.'

She flicked her long eyelashes. The ready smile was aimed at Vickery, silently urging him to accept the offer. Jolene was well aware, even if her husband was not, that the sheriff had a soft spot for her. But her persuasive wiles were not needed.

Pot Roast Charlie Cobb, the second chef at the Imperial Diner, did the job for her. 'Mrs. Wishart is right, Sheriff. We need to stop for some grub.' He sought support from his pal. 'Ain't that so, Slim?'

A stocky jigger boasting the whimsical handle of Slim Jim Picket took the bait. 'There ain't nothing likely to fire up a man's spirit more than home cooked chow. I'm all for that suggestion.' The portly guy gave the sheriff a look of gluttonous drooling. 'Don't you fellas agree?'

The other men were not slow in backing his assertion. 'Jefford can't get far on foot in this country. My betting is we'll catch up with him before sundown.' It was a credible argument from Jackdaw. The men eagerly fastened their hungry peepers onto the wavering lawman, giving Wink the chance to sneak out the back door of the barn.

'Guess it won't hurt to stop off awhile,' Vickery decided, much to the relief of all concerned, if only for differing reasons. 'It'll give the nags chance to rest up and we can refill our canteens. The next stage is across the *Yermo Tierra*. That's one bad piece of real estate. Ain't no other way he can go from here. The only water within three days ride is at Coyote Creek.'

The fugitive waited until the posse had been escorted across to the ranch house before angling round to the front of the barn where Patch was idly chewing on a hay bale. He saddled up quickly, leading the animal out of earshot before riding off. What Vickery had attested was right. He would have to cross the dry *Yermo* if'n he was going to find

Mangus Voya.

After leaving the Running W land he was forced to climb an ever-steeping grade. Zigzagging between broken scree, he let the horse pick a trail up towards the serrated skyline. Patch appeared to have a sixth sense when it came to finding the best route to take. That had been proved by his somehow ending up in Tularosa.

All Wink could do was keep heading in a general easterly direction towards the place where he knew the main Apache encampment was situated; that was on the far side of this arid plateau, and then across the notorious *Yermo Tierra*. He kept up a steady pace. Frequent halts were made to keep the appaloosa as fresh as was possible in the blazing heat. And all the while his canteen was being drained. His luck was in when he came across a shallow bed of water called Coyote Creek where he was able to fill his canteen.

It was already late in the day, so Wink decided this would be a good place to make camp. Some fifty yards downstream he spotted some shrivelled-up juniper trees that would make ideal kindling for a fire. There, beside the creek, he made a startling discovery – a broken prospecting cradle, and a heap of gravel tailings nearby. Somebody had clearly been hoping to discover paydirt in the vicinity.

He searched the area to see what had been unearthed. Minute fragments of silver glinted in the sinking rays of a dying sun. He was now well beyond the boundaries of the Running W section. Could this be Stoker land? Wink was still musing over the unexpected discovery when he fell asleep.

Next morning he was on the trail before sunrise to gain some distance towards his objective during the coolest part of the day. He dropped down through a choked amalgam of dry sagebrush and mesquite, which was slow going. It was a mixed blessing to finally leave the scrubland to his rear. Ahead of him lay the desert proper with barely anything to break the grim monotony of the rolling waves of sand.

He was acutely conscious of leaving a distinct trail of hoof prints in the gleaming ochre of the *Yermo*: a perfect trail for the posse to follow. There was no escape from this if'n he was going to make contact with Mangus.

It was mid-afternoon of the following day. Wink was dozing in the saddle at the time. About to descend a stone covered slope, Patch jerked him awake. Man and beast had just rounded a rocky promontory when suddenly another traveller appeared directly in their path, as if from nowhere. Wink instantly grabbed for his revolver.

The newcomer was clearly a prospector, judging by the gear strapped to the burro he was leading on foot. 'Don't shoot, mister,' he called out raising his hands. 'I didn't hear you a-coming, else I'd have called out.'

The grizzled veteran offered no threat, but Wink still maintained a close watch. 'What you doing out here in the middle of nowhere?' he posited keeping his gun steady.

'I'm heading over yonder.' He pointed back the way the fugitive had come. 'Hear tell there's been a silver strike near Tularosa and I intend to stake me a claim. They call me Long Tom Malloy. And this here's Betsy. We've been prospecting over by Church Butte.' He twiddled the ears of the burro. 'But I didn't fancy having my hair lifted by them Apaches.'

Mention of the Indians perked Wink's interest. 'Did you see them?' he asked.

The comment received a look that spoke of deep scepticism. 'Only from a distance. A fella don't want to get too close to those critters.' His gnarled features puckered with apprehension as he peered back down the trail. 'Although that smoke they're pumping out tells me Mangus is planning a major attack. And perty soon if'n my reading is correct. So if'n you're heading that way, best watch out. A man alone don't stand much chance against those savages.'

Turning his attention back to the scout, Long Tom noticed the canteen hooked over the saddle horn. 'Any chance of some water?' he croaked. 'My throat is drier than a temperance hall.'

Wink couldn't restrain a smile as he handed over the canteen. Molloy drank deep, forcing Wink to grab the bottle back. 'There's plenty of water on the far side of the badlands. I need what's left if'n I'm gonna reach Atoka Springs. Check it out for paydirt while you're there. I found an old rocker box and traces of silver, so at least you're headed in the right direction.'

'Much obliged, young fella: I'll do just that,' Molloy said, acknowledging the tip. 'So, you're really intent on going on.' The old prospector grunted. 'Seems to me like you've been chewing on locoweed, mister. Still,' he shrugged, 'I reckon a man has the right to choose where he's gonna die.' And with that upbeat remark, Long Tom Malloy departed, hauling the stubborn burro up the shallow grade.

Wink maintained a close eye on the old jasper trudging up the hill. Only when he had disappeared did he turn his attention to the way ahead. What stuck in Wink's mind about the meeting was the notion that he had been right about that paydirt. It was soon displaced by the need to reach Atoka Springs. Plodding ever onwards, the waves of heat rolling off the tops of the dunes gave the appearance of cool water. Of course it was all a chimera, his mind playing sly tricks. He knew it was a mirage, but that didn't stop him wishing and hoping for the real thing to appear out of the haze.

No such luck. His water canteen was soon empty, forcing him to suck on a pebble to produce a modicum of moisture to sustain life. The last few drops he saved for the faithful appaloosa. More and more he had to dismount to conserve the horse's flagging strength. Get cast afoot in this wilderness and his chances of survival would be considerably reduced. At one point he came across a set of prints. The discovery shook him up when, suddenly, he cottoned to the grim fact he had been walking in a circle. From then on an army compass kept him on a straight course.

NINE

A MIND MADE UP

Around the same time that Wink recognized his error of judgement, the posse had arrived at Coyote Creek. 'Looks like he made camp here,' observed a lean-limbed jasper called Klute Haydock, kicking at the cold ashes of a dead fire. 'At least we're on the right trail.'

'We might as well stay here the night, boys,' Vickery declared, stepping down. 'Water and feed the horses. Then you can get a fire going, Pot Roast. And make sure you cook up some'n better this time.'

'Why is it always me that's on chow duty?' the ill-disposed cook complained.

'That's because you were a top cookhouse Johnny during the War,' Jackdaw butted in, his ribald comment eliciting a bout of sniggering laughter from the others. 'Or so you're always bragging about.'

'An army always marches on its stomach. That's what they say, ain't it?' added Haydock. 'You're lucky I managed to shoot us a couple of gophers. All you have to do is skin and pot-roast them. That way you can live up to your name.'

'Not gopher again,' moaned a stiff-necked cowpoke called Batwing Jake, slapping at the leather chaps he always wore. 'That stuff is worse than rabbit.'

Vickery had had enough of the grumbling. 'Just get on with it, and quit your griping,' the sheriff rasped, lighting up a quirley. 'We have a long ride ahead of us tomorrow across *Yermo Tierra*, and that ain't gonna be no Sunday school picnic.'

Next morning they were up early, if not so bright-eyed, but not before the reluctant camp cook. Pot Roast was up first to set the coffee on the boil and heat up the refried beans and hardtack. An insidious smirk cracked the ugly mush as he viciously kicked the prone bodies into wakefulness. The harsh interruption to welcome slumber brought forth more grousing, scornfully ignored by the perpetrator. 'On your feet, toe rags. It's chow time.'

An hour later and they were ready to ride. Jackdaw had been scouting the vicinity and reported back that he had found Jefford's tracks. And sure enough, they were headed for the desert. Unfortunately, after an hour of following them, the trail went cold when a large expanse of grey lava bed was reached. The Malpais was the residue of an old volcano. 'Tracking across this stuff is impossible. We're gonna have to split and meet up later,' Vickery ordered. 'One of us is sure to come across his tracks.'

'I sure ain't going off on my ownsome around here with those Apaches on the rampage,' Pot Roast declared. 'This fella we're after is a trained scout. He'll outsmart guys like us easily.' Vickery sensed that the cook was becoming more of a liability than he needed. His constant grousing was likely to infect the rest of the posse.

'If'n you're so against this pursuit, then go back to Tularosa,' he said gruffly. 'But don't expect to get any payout when we return.'

'That's the best suggestion you've made since we set off on this wild goose chase,' Pot Roast averred, swinging his flagging mount around.

The others watched him go, uncertain what the future might bring with rampant Apaches on the prod. Only the thought of the promised bonus should they catch the fugitive was holding the posse together, and Vickery knew it. He needed to instil some grit into their backbones to prevent others quitting the chase.

'You all knew Cab Smollett. He was a good man,' he stressed. 'And those folks from the wagon train didn't deserve to be abandoned.' The sheriff was playing on their consciences and it appeared to be working. 'Your cousin was on that train, wasn't he, Klute?' he said, addressing the surly hardcase.

'Sure was.' Haydock's snarled reply was laced with venom. 'I can't wait to see that bastard hang.'

Vickery was pleased to see the others nodding

their agreement. 'We have a duty to bring him in and see that justice is served.' He then issued directions for each man to follow. 'We'll meet up near Atoka Springs. Hopefully by then one of us will have struck paydirt.'

Back in Tularosa, Jolene Wishart had arrived in town with her husband. Corby had a meeting with Frank Stoker regarding a loan to buy some cattle for the section he had inherited. His wife left the two men as she headed off down the street to the dressmaker from whom she had ordered some material. On the opposite boardwalk she spotted Angie Henstridge entering the Imperial Diner.

Jolene detoured across the street, entering the Diner and joining the younger woman. 'Mind if I join you, Angie?' she asked, standing beside the table. 'I have something to say that I think you really need to hear.'

A puzzled frown ribbed Angie's aquiline features. Nonetheless, she was intrigued as to what this woman she barely knew had to say, and gestured for her to sit down. 'Is it about Wink?' she said hesitantly after giving their order to the waitress.

The older woman nodded. 'He arrived at our ranch being chased by the posse. Corby, my husband, was going to hand him over, but I could sense deep down that Wink was telling the truth.'

'I felt the same way,' Angie interrupted, glad that somebody else felt as she did. 'But I had to be sure in my own mind. His actions are the only thing everybody's talking about.' The hurt etched across her face spoke of anguished indecision. Tears bubbled in her eyes. 'Frank thinks I'm going to marry him but . . .' She left the rest of the sentence unfinished.

Jolene knew exactly what she meant and finished the sentence. 'But you don't love him, do you?'

Angie reluctantly shook her head. 'I went to see Wink in jail before he broke out, hoping he would deny all the charges. But he brushed me off when I asked him to explain his side of the story.' More tears flowed. 'And now the deputy's been killed I don't know what to think.'

'I could tell by the way you reacted,' Jolene whispered quietly, trying to sooth this young girl's pain. 'You don't have to be ashamed to admit your feelings. You were the only one to express any reluctance to condemn him. I heard what you said when everybody else drowned you out.' She reached over and laid her hand across that of the distraught girl to offer her support. 'You were right to go with your instincts. When someone feels deep down in their heart that a miscarriage of justice is looming, they should not sit idly by and allow it to happen.'

A fresh hope shone out of Angie's watery eyes. 'You think he's innocent of these awful charges as well?' she pressed.

Jolene was reticent to raise the girl's expectations too high over an incident of which she had no knowledge. She waited until the waitress had brought their coffee and cinnamon cakes before continuing. 'When Corby was going to hand Wink over to the posse, I reminded him of a certain incident in his past, and that changed his mind. We managed to delay the posse at the ranch, giving him the chance to escape.' Jolene leaned in closer, fastening her penetrating gaze onto the young woman. 'What I have to tell might help determine your own course of action. I hope so.'

The event Jolene Wishart related had happened many years before in the Brazos country of west Texas. A young woman was helping her father who owned a store in the town of Sweetwater. Towards the end of business one day, two men came in and robbed him of the day's takings.

'The girl was out at the time and only heard about the awful tragedy later. Her pa was a feisty jasper and attempted to stop them.' This time it was Jolene who found herself crying as the whole sorry episode was resurrected. 'They shot him down, but managed to escape through a side door.' The older woman paused to compose herself before continuing with the harrowing tale.

On hearing the shot, a young man who her father employed as a storeman had come running through from the stockroom. He saw his boss lying on the floor, a smoking pistol by his side. The boy picked up the gun unconsciously along with some money the thieves had left when they fled.

And that was his undoing. At that very moment the head of the vigilance committee burst into the store, having also heard the shot. Seeing the boy standing over the dead body clutching a pistol and stolen money sealed his fate. He was quickly tackled

91

and disarmed. Nobody believed his ardent plea that it was all a mistake. The claim that he had disturbed the robbers, forcing them to flee was ignored in the heat of the moment.

A large crowd had gathered quickly. The mood was decidedly hostile. They were all of a mind to hang him there and then. At that time there was still no official law west of the Brazos River. Chuck Sangster, who controlled the vigilantes, declared that a trial would be held in the saloon that night. There would be no lynch law in Sweetwater. Until then the kid would be held under lock and key. The simmering mob marched him down to the lockup on the edge of town, none too pleased at being denied their macabre termination.

The girl was the only one who knew deep down in her heart that the boy was innocent. They had only been walking out for a couple of weeks, but it was enough for her to have gained more than a passing acquaintance with his true character. She determined to set him free.

While the rest of the mob were drinking themselves into an uproar of rabid bloodlust, the girl took the store wagon and drove it round behind the huddle of buildings parking up behind the lock-up. The catch securing the makeshift jail was enough to secure a prisoner, but was no match for a jemmy-yielding female stirred up enough to prevent an injustice.

Once he had been released, she covered the boy with a blanket and trundled off into the sunset quietly, never to return to Sweetwater. Jolene paused in her narration. The telling had clearly unearthed old memories long since buried away in a turbulent past. The two women sat in that diner, silently contemplating their similar situations. This time it was Angie who offered comfort and consolation.

Jolene was first to break the emotive hush. 'Corby and I were married in Hobbs before heading further west to settle around here. We started off living in an abandoned log cabin with two milk cows.' She stared hard at the younger woman. 'If you feel the same way about your man, fight for him.'

Her ardent words and the poignant unfolding had certainly made an impact, but as the two women left the diner, Angie was baffled as to how she could help clear Wink's name. He had gone on the run, pursued by a rampant posse eager for retribution. 'How can I do anything stuck here in Tularosa?' she snapped, the burning frustration causing her to appear sharp and tetchy.

Jolene understood the younger woman's dilemma. 'When the chance presents itself, you'll know what to do,' she replied, evincing decisive calm. A warm smile, a gentle squeeze of the arm, then she left to resume her visit to the dressmaker's.

Her mind full of the traumatic episode related by Jolene Wishart, Angie crossed the street in a daze, almost stumbling into Jolene's husband, who was still talking to Frank Stoker. They had been joined by Pot Roast Charlie Cobb, who was caked in dust and looking totally whacked, having just arrived back in town.

Pot Roast had wasted no time in returning to Tularosa. After filling up his canteen at Coyote Creek he had taken the most direct route through Dead Man's Canyon, avoiding Running W land altogether. His arrival back in the town was met with surprise by Frank Stoker, who immediately wanted to know the score. 'Why ain't you still with the posse?' he enquired accusingly.

'Vickery and that bunch of turkeys ain't got a snowball's chance in hell of finding that guy,' Cobb asserted to justify his abandonment of the pursuit. 'He's just leading them into the badlands. Chances are Jefford will outwit them and join up with Mangus Voya. If'n they somehow manage to survive being picked off by the Apaches, likely the lot of them will fry out there in the *Yermo*. I'd rather be frying up steaks in the Imperial kitchen any day.' With that blunt assertion, he stamped off.

'Well, if'n that lily-livered jasper ain't got the bottle to tough it out, I sure have,' Stoker rapped out. 'I'm going to catch them up. They need somebody with grit and determination to run that skunk to ground.' He hitched up his gun belt and made to step down where his horse was tethered.

That was when Jolene's final remark sang out inside her head: '*When the chance presents itself, you'll know what to do.*' She hadn't expected it to happen so soon. Yet here it was, and she was not about to throw the opportunity away. 'I'm coming with you.'

Both Corby Wishart and Stoker were taken aback by this sudden announcement. Their mouths gaped

94

wide. 'You can't come with me,' Stoker stuttered out once he had recovered from the shock. 'It's far too dangerous out there for a woman.'

'I can ride and shoot as good as any man,' she averred, holding her head high. 'I'm convinced that Wink Jefford has been falsely accused of cowardice and murder. And I want to show him that one person in this town is on his side.' Angie stood her ground, hands firmly planted on hips, delivering the categorical message that she would not be fobbed off. Her brow furrowed in puzzlement as another thought entered her head. 'Anyway, Frank, why would you want to go join the posse?'

Stoker ground his teeth, struggling to maintain his cool. He leaned forward, holding her shoulders. 'We're going to be married soon, honey, and I want to ensure we have law and order in this territory. Somebody has to make a stand against criminals and drifters like Jefford. It's my duty to do what I can. For some reason I can't figure, you've gotten it into your pretty head that he's innocent.'

But the girl was not to be swayed. The condescending tone riled her. Indeed she was more certain now than ever that this was the right course to follow. Her response was measured but potent. 'It seems to me you're taking far too much for granted, Frank.' She shook off the hands resting on her shoulders. 'I've never said that I'll marry you. Like Rachel, you have assumed something without asking me what I felt.'

Wishart had been listening intently. He now

butted in. 'If'n you folks are intent on joining the search then me and Fletch will tag along as well.' The rancher was also starting to question why Stoker was so anxious to find Jefford. His zealous involvement seemed more than just public loyalty.

TEN

PATCHWORK MIRACLE

The Sacramento mountain range finally appeared in the distance. Wink betrayed a sigh of relief. His canteen was empty. But it was another day before he staggered out of the blistering white of the *Yermo* only to find that Atoka Springs was nought but a dried up patch of dark grey sand.

With a heavy heart, Wink dragged his weary frame over to the shade of a large boulder. His eyes closed as total exhaustion claimed the parched and dried-out body. It was some time later that the whinnying from his horse jerked him out of a deadly nightmare. Once again he had been staked out. But this time there was no escape. The torture of a thousand cuts was about to begin.

Sweat would have bubbled up on his brow if the

dried out body had any moisture left. It was with mixed feelings that he rejoined the real world, thankful to have escaped the devil's kiss, but unsure if the future was any better.

The unsettling dream brought home the acute danger of his task. How would Mangus react after learning that his son had been shot? Would Wink even have time to plead his innocence? And, just as vital, would the chief be prepared to reveal who had betrayed the wagon train's course, and to what end?

Questions and more questions addled his brain, none of which had an answer. He could only trust his instinct and the potent symbolism of the sacred necklace given to him by Shinto before the boy joined his ancestors. For the present, however, the pressing need was to find another source of water. But with Atoka Springs dried up, had he enough time before the sun turned him into a shrivelled husk?

He must have slept right through the night. The sun was still low in the eastern sky when he awoke. Streaks of shimmering purple, pink and orange had been daubed on a blue canvas by some divine artist, but he was unable to appreciate the scintillating beauty the desert lands had to offer.

The snickering from his horse continued. He looked round to see Patch pawing at the sandy ground. The animal had made a small depression into which he now dipped his noble head. What happened next stunned the dazed traveller out of his lethargic torpor. When the head lifted it was caked in damp sand. Could the miracle he had prayed for have actually come to pass?

He struggled to his feet and staggered across. And, lo and behold, there was no mistake. A thin film of moisture lined the roughly scraped hole. Desperation found Wink scrabbling to enlarge the aperture. More water bubbled up. The horse must have inadvertently found the source of the spring water. Patch lapped up the cloudy sludge while his master bathed his sun-baked visage with a cooling balm of muddy sand. Much as he wanted to emulate the horse's instinct, he forced himself to wait until the water level had risen.

It took upwards of an hour before he could contain his craving no longer. Even then he knew that the dirty liquid would have to be filtered through his bandanna. Finally the heaven-sent opportunity could be resisted no longer. There was little more than half a mug full, but it tasted like the nectar of the gods. He lay back, gasping for breath; he was unable to comprehend how Patch had saved his life.

As the new waterhole filled up, so the residue sank to the bottom, allowing him to drink his fill. Another hour passed before the reinvigorated scout felt able to continue his journey. He picked a tenuous route up through the rough ground to gain the upper level of the plateau. That was when he witnessed the arrival of Sheriff Vickery. He was alone and had clearly followed the trail Wink had left. So what had happened to the rest of the posse?

Vickery fell off his horse, throwing himself into the

dark patch that was Atoka Springs, only to find it had dried up. The sheriff's horse just ambled away, its head drooping disconsolately, tongue hanging down like a lump of burnt meat. The lawman struggled to his knees before collapsing. He knew this was the end of his pursuit. Had he possessed a horse of Patch's quality, the elixir of life might well have been located hidden in the rocks. As it was, his brain had shut down.

The cold-eyed watcher gazed down on his pursuer, evincing no shred of pity. 'There but for the grace of God, or in my case a smart cayuse,' he muttered under his breath, patting the worthy equine head. All the same, he felt a grudging respect for the dogged lawman. But that didn't dull the fact that he was being hounded for accusations of murder and cowardice, both of which were totally groundless. 'You ought not to have jumped to the wrong conclusions, Sheriff.'

Turning away, he nudged the horse back into motion. His primary task now was to track down Mangus Voya. That was going to require all his skill, both as a scout and negotiator. It was a task no ordinary man would have attempted, but Wink Jefford had reasons way beyond the everyday problems most fellas grumbled about.

It was only when he had gone a hundred yards that his conscience began to prickle. Leaving a man to die like that was not Wink Jefford's way. The guy had saved him from being strung up by a lynch mob. He reined up, indecision clouding his features. A natural instinct for fair play wrestled with callous disregard for mercy.

The former assertion finally won the battle. With some degree of reluctance he swung round and headed back down to Atoka Springs. The sheriff had not moved. Nevertheless, Wink approached the supine form with caution. His near fatal clash with Shinto had taught a valuable lesson in guardedness. The man must have sensed his presence. He groaned attempting to turn over onto his back. Wink took hold of the man's holstered pistol and tossed it aside. No sense in tempting fate.

Vickery could barely speak. His mouth was blistered and raw. Wink dribbled water into the dry mouth, causing Vickery to grab hold of the canteen as he glugged down the precious liquid avidly. 'Not so fast, Sheriff,' he cautioned, pulling it away. 'Too much at once will give you bad stomach cramps. Best to take it easy.' He helped the man to his feet and led him into the shade.

When he had recovered sufficiently, Vickery was quick to enquire how the fugitive had managed to conserve his water supply. 'With Atoka Springs all dried to a frazzle, nobody could have traversed that wasteland and still have water left,' he charged. 'How did you manage it?' He was genuinely intrigued.

'No mystery, Sheriff,' Wink replied, gesturing for the lawman to look behind him where Patch was lapping contentedly. 'My horse discovered the point where the underground creek neared the surface.'

Vickery's eyes widened on seeing the small pool.

'Boy, you sure have one mighty sharp animal there.' Patch snickered his agreement. The two men laughed. 'He even seems to understand what we're saying.'

Wink went on to relate how the horse had found its way to Tularosa and been acquired by Corby Wishart of the Running W. 'His wrangler caught me trying to steal it back just before you and the posse arrived.'

'So you were there when Wishart claimed not to have seen you?' The lawman was none too pleased at having been duped by the rancher. 'Why in thunder-ation did he do that?'

'Don't blame him.' Wink was quick to defend the rancher's actions. He had no wish to see him ostra-cized, or even arrested for conspiring to break the law. 'His wife had the good sense to recognize that the story I told them was the darned truth. Some inci-dent happened in their past that persuaded him to help me out by delaying you while I got away.'

Ever the doughty badgeholder, Troy Vickery was not about to give up his quest. 'Just 'cos you helped me out don't mean I won't keep on your trail. Far as I'm concerned you're still guilty of murdering my deputy. That stuff about abandoning the wagon train ain't my concern now.' His eyes glittered with deter-mination to perform his duty, no matter what.

'You're a tough man, Sheriff.' Wink sighed, but nevertheless he gripped his revolver a mite tighter.

'Hard but fair. All I want is to see justice carried out,' was the curt reply. The two men held each other

102

in a fixed gaze.

Wink's brain was musing on how to swing the lawman's resolve in his direction. Then a thought struck him. His eyes lit up. 'Remember when you first locked me up?' Vickery gave the query a slow nod. 'You removed my guns . . . and the bone handled bowie knife I was carrying.'

Another nod of agreement. 'What you getting at, fella?'

The weapon in question was then removed from the sheath attached to his gun belt. 'This it?' He didn't wait for an answer. 'I grabbed the rig when Shinto rescued me. It was his knife you found in Cab Smollett's back, not mine. Ain't that proof it was the Indian who killed your deputy?'

Vickery prided himself on being an impartial officer of the law. He was always prepared to listen and way up the pros and cons of an argument, unlike hotheaded jiggers like Frank Stoker who jumped in with both feet without weighing the odds. He stood up and moved away, thinking on what he had just been told. 'It certainly puts the evidence in your favour,' he mused. 'But that doesn't stop you being an accessory. Come back to Tularosa with me and I'll make sure to argue your case in a court of law.'

'Not a chance, Sheriff,' Wink scoffed. 'You managed to keep that mob off'n me last time. I ain't about to risk my neck again.' He mounted up. 'I'm taking your horse and guns and going after Mangus to clear my name. He's the only one who can tell me who really betrayed those folks.'

103

'You can't leave me here without any protection,' Vickery protested.

'Guess you're right at that,' Wink relented, untying the saddle pack and tossing it down. 'You have water and enough trail grub until the rest of the posse get here. When they do I'd suggest you all turn back. If'n we meet up again I won't be so generous.'

One final thing was still puzzling the scout. 'How did you manage to track me across the lava beds?' Wink enquired ever respectful of a good tracker. 'I deliberately crossed there to lose you.'

Vickery shrugged. 'No skill on my part, just luck, I guess. After leaving Stoker land at Coyote Creek, we split up.'

Wink's eyes widened as he quickly butted in. 'You saying that Coyote Creek is owned by Frank Stoker?' A quizzical nod from the lawman found Wink removing the sample of silver ore from his pocket. 'I found this at a spot upstream where somebody had been prospecting.'

A brief examination had the lawman issuing a low whistle of surprise. 'Looks like this could be a rich vein. Frank Stoker has gotten himself a lucky break inheriting that land from his brother.'

Wink's face hardened into a bleak look of denunciation. The noxious truth was beginning to unfold. Before he could voice his grim conclusion, a harsh rasp to his rear curtailed any more thought of continuing his quest. 'Raise your hands, Jefford. Any funny business and it'll be your last.'

Jackdaw had heard the muted conversation after

discovering the dried out spring. A covert foray revealed that their quarry had turned the tables. The tracker was dead on his feet but from his hidden vantage point, it appeared that the sheriff and Jefford were anything but. A puzzled scowl found him backing off. How had they managed to beat the blistering heat? The conundrum was shelved when the others arrived and he frantically gestured for them to remain close-mouthed. Not that the dry spring gave them anything to crow about.

Only the corpulent Slim Jim Picket was missing. He had been forced to stop and dig a stone out his nag's hoof. Being the first to reach their destination, Jackdaw assumed command. 'We'll take the skunk by surprise and see what the sheriff intends doing with him,' he asserted, leading the way as they sneaked round to confront the alleged killer.

The sudden challenge came as a severe jolt to Wink's plans. He had been well and truly suckered. 'You take his gun, Batwing.' Jackdaw's eyes latched onto the small waterhole. His mouth opened, unable to believe what he was seeing.

'Go ahead, boys,' declared an upbeat Troy Vickery retrieving his own revolver. 'It's good water. This fella's horse sussed it out.' The three posse men staggered over and threw themselves down, slurping at the life-giving elixir.

'You sure had me fooled into thinking you were alone, Vickery,' Wink grunted, more angry with himself for assuming too much. 'I should have done what I intended and left you for the buzzards.'

Vickery puckishly tapped his nose 'A good lawman always keeps an ace up his sleeve,' the sheriff preened, thoroughly delighted with his subterfuge. 'You may have persuaded me that you didn't kill my deputy, but that's still for a court to decide. I'm taking you back.'

But Klute Haydock had other ideas. 'This bum was responsible for the death of my kin and those other poor devils.' He grabbed the rope from his horse. 'I say we string the yellow rat up by his heels and drill him full of lead. Save the town the expense of a trial. You with me, boys?' Batwing and Jackdaw were less than enthusiastic to take the law into their own hands, but they went along with Haydock's grim premise.

Vickery's gun shifted to cover the irate Haydock. 'As I told you back in Tularosa, there'll be no lynching while I'm in charge of this posse. Jefford saved my life out there, and I'll shoot any darned critter that tries to take him.' Both men stood their ground, eyeing one another.

The confrontation was defused by the sudden outburst of gunfire beyond the cover of the rocks. In the flick of a gnat's tongue the grim reality of their precarious situation struck home. They all rushed to the narrow gap giving onto the dry spring. A rider was galloping headlong across the open tract of sand. It was Slim Jim Picket. Puffs of smoke from a dozen rifles could be seen on the rocky rim to his left.

'Come on, Slim, you can make it!' shouted Jackdaw, willing the bulky rider to reach the safety of their rocky enclave. Picket was halfway across when his horse buckled under the fusillade of shots. Apparently unhurt, the jasper scrambled to his feet and stumbled towards where his buddies were waving their hands. And he might have made it but for his cumbersome gait. Three bullets slammed into his back, bringing the desperate race to a brutal finale from which there was no return.

Fury gripped the trapped men. They immediately responded with panic-induced pistol and rifle fire, which had no effect on the hidden Apaches. Only Wink could see the futility of their inept actions. 'Don't waste your ammunition. That's what they want,' he exhorted. 'They have all the time in the world. Ain't nobody within three days ride of here to come riding to the rescue.'

'He's right, boys,' Vickery concurred. 'We're gonna need every bullet with all those red devils out there.'

'But you've forgotten that we have the new water supply,' Batwing Jake contended smugly. 'They can see that the spring is dry. So we can hold them off until they realize there ain't no easy pickings here.'

Wink was not so optimistic. 'I wouldn't be so sure. This is Apache territory. Mangus knows every rock there is. Apaches are patient. But he'll want to get this over with fast now he knows the spring is dry. Soon they'll begin moving in under cover picking us off one at a time.' His ardent gaze fastened onto each of the trapped posse men. 'We're in a tight spot. But there is one possible way out of this pickle.'

ELEVEN

PLAYING POSSUM

They all looked towards the scout for his direction. Anything that might save their skins was worth considering. All thoughts of their reason for joining the posse in the first place had been thrust aside. Now it was a matter of personal survival. Wink posed a question. 'What does a possum do when he's threatened?'

The frightened men looked nervously at each other. It was the irascible Klute Haydock who cut to the chase. 'Don't play games with us, mister. Just tell us what you're getting at. And make it snappy.'

The petulant retort was to conceal his own trepidation, and Wink knew it. He eyed the quaking hardcase with barely concealed disdain. 'Just think about it. A possum lies down and plays dead, hoping his enemy will leave him be. That's his way of surviving an attack from a predator. And we should do the

108

same.' He looked round the blank faces ghoulishly, enjoying their confusion.

This time it was Jackdaw who expressed his impatience. 'We don't need a nature lesson, mister. Just get to the crunch.'

'It's simple. We put on a show by staggering out there and slump down in that dried up pan. Figuring that we're all gasping out our last breath will draw Mangus into the open. Then we can let them have it.' A grizzly smirk followed. 'And that, gents, is what we call playing possum.' He waited as they tossed over the plan in their fearful minds, weighing up the chances of coming out of this pickle with a whole skin.

'I ain't going out there for a gutful of lead,' Haydock objected vehemently.

Wink shrugged. 'So I take it you've come up with a better plan?' To that query the big mouth had no answer. He looked away, shuffling his feet uncomfortably. 'I thought not,' Wink rasped. But none of the others was prepared to make the first move. 'Well, if'n you critters ain't gotten the bottle, best give me my gun back.' He held out his hand. Vickery returned the Colt Frontier, making sure to keep his own weapon cocked and ready for any skulduggery.

'Don't worry, Sheriff,' he said caustically. 'I ain't gonna pull no tricks. He's after my hair just as much as your'n.' He went over to where Patch was fraternizing with the other horses. 'You and me have some serious work to do, fella.'

His final order to the greenhorn combatants was

bluntly terse. 'When the shooting starts, leave Mangus to me. I want to take him alive to reveal the true culprit of that massacre.'

The narrowed gaze, cold and deliberate, held the men in a grip of iron. Satisfied that his point had been driven home, he staggered out into the open, giving the impression that a deadly thirst was gripping him. Sharp eyes could pick out the Indian presence on the far rim of the enclosing circlet of rocks. He prayed hard that his unexpected appearance would draw no violent response. Silence hung heavy as he slumped to the ground and lay still.

'It's your turn now, heroes,' he hissed over his shoulder. 'And make it look good.' The scout's successful trickery had bolstered the courage of the posse, who now likewise emerged from hiding to give a similar display. Soon the five human possums were lying still. Wink prayed that the ruthless chief had been hoodwinked by the ruse.

Mangus waited a full thirty minutes, which did nothing for the nerves of the apprehensive pretenders. 'You sure this is gonna work?' Vickery muttered. 'Stay here for much longer under this sun and we'll be fried to a crisp anyway.'

'They're here now,' Wink replied cautiously, signalling for them all to lie doggo. 'Nobody move until I give the word. And remember, leave Mangus to me.' The blunt command was not to be ignored, as they all fully appreciated. But it was clear that the bulk of the Apache force had remained hidden, ready to attack should the need arise. Mangus was playing a cautious game, but couldn't resist being in the vanguard of the attack to increase his reputation as a fearless leader.

The Mimbrano chief approached the supine forms guardedly. Wink could hear various grunted remarks as they drew ever closer. A wary eye remained open as he watched, hardly daring to breath. Mangus gave the signal for his braves to draw their skinning knives. A rictus of hate soured the leathery face as the merciless chief led the eager scalp hunters forward.

That was the moment Wink shouted for the action to commence. 'OK, let them have it, boys.' His gun barked twice, taking one brave down.

The rest of the group suddenly came alive. The Indians had been taken completely by surprise. But they soon recovered, seeking cover among the surrounding rocks. Elated at their initial success, Batwing Jake hawked out a gleeful *yeeehaaa!* But in doing so, he raised himself too far above the parapet and paid the price for his folly. All the others could do was blast away at anything with black hair tied back in a headband.

The unexpected resistance of the defenders forced Mangus back onto the defensive. A growl of rage spat from the Mimbreno chief's throat. But he had the advantage of numbers so any uncertainty was only fleeting. The battle was resumed with greater intensity as more braves were called down to join the attack. Fortune had favoured the underdogs in the form of the dried up depression, which gave them

111

some protection. And they made full use of it.

On the downside, an almost insurmountable obstacle: there were now only four of them up against a formidable band of bloodthirsty renegades. Such long odds did not auger well for their continued survival. Wink was well aware that Mangus would send snipers out to pick them off at random. Unless Lady Luck smiled down, it was only a matter of time before they would be overrun. But he kept these morbid reflections to himself. It would take time for the snipers to get into position. No sense in causing a panic.

The deadly clash continued apace. A couple more Indians went down, which buoyed up the morale of the defenders. Mangus sensed that he had lost the initiative and called off his men, retreating back to their enclave. The defenders of Atoka Springs jumped up, whistling and yarroping at having defeated the enemy. 'We sure showed those red devils that one white man is worth a dozen Apaches,' Klute Haydock scoffed. 'I reckon they've had enough and skidaddled back to their holes.'

But Wink was far more circumspect. 'Mangus won't give up that easy,' he mused, keeping a watchful eye on the escarpment. 'He'll be after avenging the death of his son. This is one of his ploys: to let us think he's been beaten. When our resistance is down, he'll attack with his whole force. In the meantime, keep your heads down and watch out for snipers.'

That piece of unwelcome logic quickly removed the smiles of victory. 'So what can we do?' Jackdaw muttered disconsolately, casting a troubled look towards the bloody corpse of Batwing Jake.

'Make sure every shot counts and pray for a miracle,' was the only advice Wink could offer. 'At least we've gotten water. All we can do now is wait.'

And waiting they were forced to do. Wink was used to it, but nerves were getting the better of the others. Haydock especially was becoming fractious and jumpy. 'Come on, you bunch of yellow snakes,' he railed impotently at the hidden foe. 'What you waiting for? Come out of your holes and face some real opposition.'

As if in answer to his challenge, a mass of riders burst from cover on the far side of the hollow. A-whooping and a-hollering, faces painted up, they thundered down on the meagre foe. The chances were stacked against the defenders. Their ammunition was running low. Survival would soon be a matter of hand-to-hand combat, for which Apaches were renowned. Panic and desperation gripped their innards.

Jackdaw was the first to go down. The riddled body flopped down next to Klute Haydock, who shivered in horror before frantically emptying his pistol at Mangus. They were panic-induced shots, only one of which struck the chief in the chest. The lucky shot punched Mangus off his pony. Wink cursed the hard-case, but could do nothing for the present while the attack was still in full swing.

The wounded chief dragged himself to one side, but it was clear to Wink that he was badly injured.

Would he survive long enough for them to drive off the rest? Seeing their leader stricken, the surviving braves retreated back to their hidden camp to lick their wounds. This was proving harder than they had expected.

And it was all due to the resourceful influence of Wink Jefford. Without their leader, the Indians lacked the spirit and drive to continue the fight. Like headless chickens, they milled around unsure what to do next.

A brave called Coronadas, the chief's brother, took the initiative, urging them to follow him in one final assault to destroy the hated white eyes and retrieve the body of the fallen Mangus Voya. 'Come, stir yourselves, brave warriors of the Mimbreno tribe, and avenge the fall of our great chief,' the doughty Indian decreed fervently. 'We owe my brother's earthly spirit the chance to join his ancestors by shedding the blood of his enemy. Follow me now and victory will be ours.'

The brave's passionate oratory had the desired effect of reversing the rebels' waning fortitude, thus stimulating a fresh wave of ardour. Now that his brother was dead, Coronadas had ambitions to take over as chief. Led by the determined aspirant, the final charge was launched. The ground shook with the pounding of a dozen horses, alerting the three survivors.

'Looks like this is gonna be the last stand,' Wink declared stoically. 'Make sure we go down fighting.' Both the sheriff and Klute Haydock stared hard at the plucky scout, their faces displaying a hefty measure of respect. These were neither the words nor the actions of a coward who had abandoned his duty.

'We're with you all the way,' Vickery said, joining Wink. 'Ain't we, Klute?' Haydock dropped down beside him in support. 'Sorry for not believing in you, mister,' he timorously apologized. 'You've proved beyond doubt there's steel in your veins.' He held out a hand. The gesture was reciprocated with a coy smile as the charging Apaches bore down on them.

They were halfway across the open sward when, all of a sudden, the hurtling charge stumbled to a halt. Unsettled horses milled about in confusion as arms pointed towards the west. They had clearly spotted something detrimental to their cause. The attack was abandoned as they turned about and disappeared back into the hills.

TWELVE

A STARTLING REVELATION

Vickery was the first to notice what had so alarmed the Indians. A cloud of dust could be seen rising over a low rise. It had to be a friendly faction coming to their rescue, with shots from the liberators urging the fleeing Indians to ditch their quest, although it was impossible to determine how many riders the group comprised.

'It must be an army patrol that has scared them off,' remarked a jubilant Klute Haydock. Only when they came into view was it clearly evident that rather than the hefty force anticipated there were only four in the group. The dust had concealed their numbers.

Surprise mingled with relief as the blurred outline of the approaching rescue party revealed Corby Wishart and his wrangler Fletch. Wink scowled on recognizing the third rider as the hotheaded Frank Stoker. Identification of the fourth member hidden beneath a wide-brimmed grey Stetson was forgotten with exhilaration and relief abounding as the belea-guered survivors greeted the rescue party.

'You guys appeared in the nick of time,' the sheriff declared. 'If'n that last Apache charge hadn't been cut short by your appearance we'd surely all have been dead ducks by now.'

'It was the arrival of Pot Roast Cobb and his claim that you were struggling to catch Jefford that per-suaded me to come and help out,' Stoker asserted, stepping forward to confront Wink. 'Seems like you did find the murdering skunk after all. Now we can take him back to face a judge and jury.' A cold atmos-phere had suddenly fallen over the elation of moments before.

Virulent animosity oozing from every pore of the incensed landowner precipitated the fourth member of the group into the forefront of the tense gather-ing. Startled looks were aimed her way on realizing that a woman had come along. 'What in tarnation are you doing here, Angie?' Vickery blurted out. 'This ain't no situation for a woman to be in.'

Stoker butted in. 'I couldn't stop her. She was determined to come along no matter what I said.'

Angie elbowed her way forward. She had no inten-tion of being snubbed. 'I was convinced in my own mind that this man is innocent of all those charges. And I came to tell him so in person.' A passionate gaze was fixed onto the scout, willing him silently to

117

respond in a like manner. A fleeting smile, the sinuous exchange of reciprocated feeling passing between the two was lost on Frank Stoker. The guy's sole aim was to dispose of this meddlesome interloper.

'You're just letting foolish emotion rule your head,' Stoker declared, trying to suppress her assertion. 'Everything points to him being in league with the Apaches. And you can't say he didn't kill Smollett while busting out of jail with that Indian.'

That was the moment Sheriff Vickery decided to make his presence felt. 'What you're alleging ain't exactly true, Frank,' he declared with conviction. 'Jefford here has given me proof he had nothing to do with the killing of my deputy. I don't know about him being in league with Indians. It sure didn't seem that way when he saved my bacon and helped us defend ourselves when they attacked.'

The object of their heated exchange had been keeping a watchful eye on the one person who could have cleared up the confusion once and for all. But Mangus Voya was lying out in the open, his spirit now apparently communing with those of his ancestors. Then the unimaginable happened: Wink saw the dead body move. He blinked and looked again. There was no question. Mangus was still breathing. He had shifted and was now attempting to raise himself.

'There's the jasper who can clear this business up once and for all,' he blurted out, hurrying across to the stricken rebel. Firmly, but with care, he helped

118

the chief to his feet, half-carrying him across to the new spring. There he bathed the drawn features, dribbling water between dry lips. The Mimbreno chief was hauled up into a sitting position, back resting against a slab of rock. 'Tell me, oh great one, who was it who betrayed the wagon train of the settlers?' Wink pressed, eager for the badly wounded Indian to reveal his secret.

Mangus was barely alive. Haggard and drawn, his rasping breath informed everyone present that the end was nigh. The hard face creased up as a barb of pain shot through his dying frame. It was clear, however, from the scornful glower that he had no wish to help these white invaders. 'Let me die and go to join the spirit of my son,' he gasped out. 'There is nothing I can tell you.'

Stoker visibly sighed, his tense body relaxing. But Wink was not about to give up now. He lifted the silver and turquoise amulet given him by Shinto and held it up for the Indian to behold. 'Your son gave me this before he passed on,' Wink enunciated clearly and slowly to ensure the chief understood. 'It was hidden beneath his shirt. How could I have secured it without his consent?'

The glassy look widened on recognition of this most potent of Mimbreno symbols glittering in the harsh sunlight. A tremulous hand reached out and clutched the precious icon to his chest. His eyes closed as if in prayer before opening slowly. The rheumy gaze fastened onto the man before him. 'It is as you say, white man. You must indeed have been

119

friend to my son.'

'So tell me, for Shinto's sake,' Wink paused to get the dying man's full attention. 'Who betrayed the settlers?'

Those gathered round in this remote desert oasis held their breath, leaning forward to learn the answer to this dilemma. Angie, in particular, was on edge. She caught hold of Wink's hand. He squeezed it, staring deep into the very soul of Mangus Voya, urging him silently to come clean.

The dying Apache shifted his position, looking round at the assembled watchers. His faltering gaze came to rest on Frank Stoker. An arm lifted as a pointing finger swung towards the real perpetrator of the heinous carnage. Then he fell back, clutching his son's sacred relic. A smile graced the leathery face as he went to join him.

The dying revelation had left them all in shock. All except Frank Stoker who already knew he was in deep trouble. Yet still he tried to refute the charge tossed his way. 'Surely you don't believe what some ignorant savage says on his deathbed. It's all lies.' But the accusing looks clearly told him that his claim of innocence had fallen on deaf ears.

'Why, Frank?' Angie pleaded. 'How could you send your own kin and all those others to their deaths? It doesn't make any sense.'

'I'll tell you why,' Wink hissed, his tone measured and yet full of rancour as he removed the chunk of ore from his jacket and held it up for all to see. 'He'd discovered there was a rich vein of silver on his land

and wanted it all for himself.' Wink's tone hardened as he stepped forward. 'And I was the ideal patsy to take the blame. Ain't that right, Frank?'

Stoker didn't wait for the inevitable adverse reaction from his associates. His gun swung to cover the stunned group as he backed away towards his horse. He knew that a hangman's rope awaited him back in Tularosa if'n he stuck around any longer. Out the corner of his eye he spotted Fletcher Boon reaching for his own pistol. Stoker's shooter blasted, removing the threat with a bullet to the heart.

Angie screamed as Stoker grabbed her round the waist. She struggled to free herself, receiving a cuff round the head from the man who claimed to have loved her. It had all been a charade, a false front. All he had ever wanted was the wealth and prestige that a rich silver strike would bring. She had merely been the icing on the cake, a pretty bauble to flaunt. Gone was the urbane self-assurance; the truly ruthless character of a cold despot was now revealed in all its ugly malevolence.

Right from the beginning, Wink Jefford had seen through the thinly daubed guise of cultured sophistication that Frank Stoker had tried to assume ineptly. Yet even he was stunned when the hideous reality was revealed.

'I'm clearing out,' the braggart snarled, backing towards his horse and forcing the terrified girl to mount up in front of him. 'Anybody who follows will be sealing her fate. I ain't got nothing to lose now.' He spurred off, despatching a couple of bullets towards the hovering posse to show he meant business.

'He can't get far riding double on a tired horse,' Wink declared, hurrying across to where Patch was nuzzling the mare of his choice. 'No time for that now, fella,' he chided the proud stallion playfully. 'We have urgent work to do.'

Corby Wishart joined him. 'I'll tag along in case the skunk pulls any tricks,' the rancher said, eager to avenge his wrangler's untimely shooting. 'Fletch was more than just an employee. We'd been together a long time. He didn't deserve that.'

Wink sought to temper the rancher's fervent suggestion. 'Stoker will likely know he can't out-distance any pursuit with the girl in tow. My figuring is that when they're out of sight, he'll ditch her. I need you to bring her back here.' A raised hand silenced the protestation. 'Your horse is tuckered out as well.' Wink had no wish to demean the older man; the conciliatory tone that followed softened the rebuff. 'As an ex-army scout I work better alone. And we all know this guy is pure poison.'

Wishart concurred reluctantly. 'You make sure to catch that scumbag and bring him back to stand trial. Or over a saddle if'n needs be.'

Wink nodded as he headed off, watched by a bald eagle circling high above on the hot thermals. The bird's impartial gaze shifted to the fleeing bad hat. A scowl of frustration graced the warped features of the disgraced Judas. Bitter regret at not having pushed through a lynching in Tularosa when he had the chance was reflected starkly by the twisted snarl he was giving his unwelcome passenger. He could not deny that Angie Henstridge was one classy dame but, just like she had surmised, she was only ever intended as eye candy to enhance a respectable front for his clandestine activities. That had been tossed out with the bath water now. And it was all due to that interfering scout.

Stoker's devious brain had been running along similar lines to those of Jefford. The girl was a burden he could well do without. So at the earliest opportunity after he had disappeared from view round the next low knoll, Angie was dumped unceremoniously.

'Finding you here will slow that coyote up and give me the chance to disappear,' he said, scoffing at the poor girl's tear-streaked countenance. 'Quit that blubbering. You've gotten what you wanted. And he's welcome to you. Adios, honey.' And with that acerbic retort, he dug down and galloped off in a cloud of dust.

Angie slumped to the ground, barely able to comprehend what was happening. How had her life come down to this sorry state of affairs? She was not alone for long, however. Five minutes later the sound of hoof beats found her scrambling to her feet. Relief pushed aside any self-pity when Wink Jefford swung into view. He was accompanied by Corby Wishart, who was leading her own mount, but Angie's whole being was focused on the scout.

Immediately he jumped off his horse and she was

in his arms. Tears flowed as she clung desperately to the tough, wiry frame. No words were spoken, such was her thankfulness for his presence. Her head was buried in his chest as she clung on, not ever wanting to let go.

Wink was similarly affected by the emotive reunion. Nevertheless, he knew that matters of a more level-headed nature needed his urgent attention. Gently, he prised open the girl's fierce grip. 'You're safe now, Angie. And nobody is going to take you away from me again.'

Her head lifted, hope writ large in those deep-set blue eyes. 'You feel the same?' She didn't wait for a reply. 'How can you forgive me for ever doubting you? It was Frank who planted all those lies in my head. I should never have been taken in by his underhanded baloney.' Again she clung to him, offering her lips.

Wink was sorely tempted. But he managed to resist. A brief kiss then he pulled away. 'This isn't over yet by a long chalk. I have to go after the varmint and bring him back. . . .'

'But he might kill you,' Angie intervened, anxious not to lose this man again. 'He's already got blood on his hands and will be desperate enough to do anything to escape justice.'

But Wink's mind was made up. 'He's the only one who can prove beyond doubt that I had nothing to do with that massacre. I need him to stand trial with the sheriff and Corby acting as witnesses to his admission of guilt. There's too many folks in Tularosa still

124

think I'm the culprit.' His ardent gaze urged her to accede to the logic of his reasoning. 'You do understand, don't you? It's the only way.'

Reluctantly, she agreed. The rancher had stood back, somewhat embarrassed by this overt display of affection. With the verbal exchange now back on the more practical ground he understood, Corby voiced his own support of the scout's decision. 'He's right, Angie. You'd never be able to settle down together with these charges hanging over his head.'

Time was slipping away with Stoker getting further away. The moment to leave was now an urgent priority. Wink mounted up. Patch snickered his accord, eager to get on with the chase. 'You look after her, Corby,' Wink said. 'I'll be back afore you know it, along with that double-crosser.'

'Dead or alive, son. It don't matter none to me. The sheriff and me will back you up,' the rancher remarked, adding a note of caution. 'Just make sure that you're the one still breathing if'n it comes to the crunch.'

'I sure will, buddy.' And with a brisk wave he galloped off. The two people watched him until he had rounded the next bend, both praying fervently that he would indeed return.

THIRTEEN

ACROSS THE GREAT DIVIDE

Going after a wanted felon who had nothing to lose would require all of Wink's concentration. Allow his guard to drop for a second and that could be the last breath he drew on this earth. It was a daunting prospect, but the scout was experienced in such matters, having hunted down Indian renegades for the army. That said, pursuing a lone white man was a more thorny matter entirely.

Indians possessed a different mentality when engaging their enemies where prestige and honour figured highly. Status was often far more important than the actual reason for the conflict. Also, the adoption of magic totems and symbols, allegedly making them invincible, encouraged more life-threatening risks. Most potent and the ultimate accolade, however, was to count coup where merely touching a foe and escaping unscathed would confer tribal honour on the participant.

White men, on the other hand, were far more practical, placing all their faith in a good reliable firearm. Tactics and strategy played an important role in achieving success in battle. Pursuit of Frank Stoker would be a forthright man-to-man battle. Survival would depend on guile, cunning and devious trickery where anything went to achieve the ultimate goal of defeating your adversary.

Wink was under no illusions that Stoker would resort to any means, fair or foul, to defeat his tracker. Honour and justice played no part in his mission to avoid capture. Accordingly, therefore, Wink needed to remain alert at all times. Hawkish eyes scanned the wild terrain constantly. This was especially vital during these early stages of the hunt in broken country where his quarry could be hiding behind any available cover. The upshot meant that he was unable to press Patch to a full gallop, unlike Stoker who would be stretching his mount to the limit.

That might well be the skunk's downfall as his horse was much less rested than his pursuer. Panic to distance himself from Atoka Springs would be an all-consuming passion. That was the hope that buoyed the scout up. A steady yet relentless canter found him heading into more sandy terrain dominated by low stands of catclaw and sagebrush. And that was where he spotted the telltale signs that he was closing the gap. A distinct swirl of dust some two miles ahead had to have been made by the fugitive.

Satisfaction of running his quarry to ground brought a tight smile to the hard features. Soon it would all be over. Wink had no doubts of a successful end to his vengeful quest. Determination to vindicate his sullied reputation was writ large across the stoical facade. And by heading out into the dry wilderness of the *Yermo Tierra*, Stoker was playing right into his hands. A tired horse and being short on water would prove to be his undoing.

Now boasting the ignominious label of a discredited snake-in-the-grass, Stoker knew he was in deep trouble. The villain had similarly noted the dust cloud revealing the presence of his nemesis but, unlike Wink, he was more cognisant of the local terrain. He paused, the devious brain working out a plan to thwart capture. Continuing on his present course across the desert would lead him into the jaws of certain death, or surrender, which was equally dire.

The only way forward was to head for the mountains.

Two miles behind, Wink could now clearly see man and horse up ahead. And they had come to a halt. He slowed to a walk, a ribbed brow puzzling over this unexpected outcome. Was the guy ready to give up? The static profile was silhouetted starkly against the brilliant white of the arid plain. The pursuer also halted, waiting, wondering.

Stuck in the middle of this bleak wilderness, the two antagonists sat their mounts, each mulling over their options from differing angles. Five minutes passed with no movement from either participant in this bleak game of chase. The heat was intense out there in the open, doubly so when reflected back off the harsh white of the unforgiving desert.

Unfurling his necker, Wink daubed the sweat from his face, applying the soothing dampness to Patch's muzzle. The horse snickered with appreciation. A puckered frown saw him muttering to the patient horse under his breath. 'Now what do you suppose that critter is up to?'

It was Stoker who made the first move. He swung his horse at right angles to the line of travel, picking up the pace and heading directly for the stark upthrust of the Sacramentos. The unexpected deviation took Wink by surprise. From his vantage point atop a low knoll, the harsh line of cliffs looked impregnable. Only a mountain goat could climb up there. The angle of the sun illuminated the orange sandstone, turning it to a blazing inferno. A shiver ran through the taut frame. It was now evident that Stoker's intention was to attempt the impossible, knowing that he had nothing to lose. Wink knew he had no choice but to follow in his wake.

It was around five miles to the base of the craggy upsurge. Stoker was pushing his horse to the limit. He knew from the increasingly laborious gait that the animal was nearing the end of its endurance. 'Come on, you mangy nag,' he berated the struggling cayuse. 'Just get me to those rocks over yonder.' He was still a hundred yards short when the lather-spat-tered chestnut, blood dribbling from its flanks from the vicious spurring, stumbled and fell, pitching its rider onto the ground.

A rabid curse found the owlhoot scrambling to his feet. He aimed a vicious kick at the worn-out beast, any sympathy being reserved for his own precarious situation. Now that he was on foot, a quick glance to his rear saw his pursuer closing the gap rapidly.

The Winchester carbine was snatched from its boot. He then hurriedly traversed the intervening flat sandy stretch, grateful to lose himself in the amalgam of large boulders at the base of the tower-ing rock face. 'Up here is where you're gonna get your comeuppance, hotshot,' he snarled as the ascent began. Stoker had no trouble locating the narrow grooved track snaking across the cliff face at an angle. It blended into the orange fracturing of the bare rock, impossible to see from below.

The climb was stiff and exceedingly dangerous, having been previously used by agile Indians hunting goats and deer. That was how Stoker had first discov-ered it whilst on a hunting expedition. The tribe had long since been driven further west into the inner mountain fastness. All his attention was required to avoid a fatal slip that would plunge him over the edge.

As he climbed ever higher, numerous back glances told him that his pursuer was doggedly stick-ing to his tail. The ugly smirk indicated that he had no fear of being caught. In this pitiless terrain he was the master. 'Just keep a-coming, mister, and you'll soon discover that the hunter will become the hunted.'

Far below, Wink's horse had stopped beside the dying chestnut mare. The stallion knew the horse was in its latter stages. A pitiful snicker offered sympathy as Patch sniffed the trembling body. The mare tried to raise her head but the effort was too much. Wink sighed. Once again he was being called on to put an animal out of its misery. This time his gun carried out the unwholesome task. There was no need for silence. Patch's foot pawed at the twitching corpse.

'Best thing for the poor gal,' Wink murmured into the stallion's ear. 'But I still have work to do, so you're gonna have to stick around.' He walked the horse over to the cluster of rocks at the base of the cliff wall and found a shaded spot where small areas of tough grama grass had managed to flourish.

Once Patch was settled, Wink stood back and peered up at the fractured edifice, but could observe no movement. 'I know you're up there somewhere,' he mumbled to himself, extracting a pair of binoculars from his saddlebag. Focusing in brought the brutal upthrust into stark yet transparent relief. A methodical pan across the cliff face soon picked out the narrow ledge slanting diagonally across. By following it up his keen eyes were soon able to pick out a tiny figure half way up the narrow trail. 'Gotcha!' he exclaimed aloud, punching out an elated cry of satisfaction.

Then began the laborious climb following in the

wake of his adversary.

But what one person could see from below, another had a much more expansive panorama from above. By leaning out gingerly over the edge of the shelf, Stoker was able to spot his pursuer just beginning the arduous climb. He coughed out a mocking guffaw. 'Think you've gotten me trapped, eh? Well, you're gonna be in for the surprise of your life.' Another honking chortle and he turned back to continue the precarious ascent.

There was no rush. He had sufficient time for what he had in mind. On reaching the top of the cliff, the terrain became much easier. From here on there was no clear trail, so it was necessary for the wily trickster to ensure his pursuer experienced no difficulty in following. Just enough to make him believe the fugitive was becoming careless due to the panic-stricken need to escape retribution.

A half-mile further and the level mesa suddenly terminated in a deep chasm. Far below, a thousand feet or more, could be seen a narrow creek, the very one that fed water into Atoka Springs. Without the fall rains to provide a decent flow it was little more than a trickle. That was of no concern to Frank Stoker, who was now praying that what he sought was still in existence.

He pushed through the strands of desiccated juniper cloaking the upper reaches soon emerging into the open. Gingerly, he approached the edge, holding his breath. The awesome rift was no more than a hundred feet across. But was the structure he sought still in existence?

A sigh of relief issued from between gritted teeth. And there it was – a rope bridge constructed by the Indians spanning the ravine. He scuttled down to the flat ledge where two supporting beams had been driven into ground cracks. The sisal rope was still in good condition. A few sharp tugs shook the whole formation with no sign of any weakness. The test would come when he traversed the awesome gap. Over a year had passed since he had first discovered the bridge.

At this angle the bottom of the ravine was in shadow. Dire thoughts of the bridge collapsing midway across caused a cold shiver to race down the schemer's backbone. At that moment a flight of doves swooped down in formation to see what was happening. They settled on the branches of some spindly mesquite bushes to watch the show.

Stoker ignored them. His whole attention was focussed on the coming traverse. A pair of buffalo hair ropes for handholding was attached by thinner connecting strands to a central walkway of bound slats: simple but effective. Stoker sucked in a lungful of hot air, girding himself for the momentous event. The need to be on the far side, awaiting his pursuer, told him this was no time for dithering. Both hands would be essential for a safe crossing, so the rifle was strapped across his back.

The initial tentative few steps onto the bridge found it shaking. A gasp escaped through pursed lips. Since his first visit, Stoker had learned that the breathtaking abyss had been named Dead Man's Drop. Now he understood why. On his first visit he had lost his nerve and turned back. No chance of that now. Hesitation laced with fear gripped his innards while trying desperately to stem the trembling in his leg muscles. Then, slowly, he began to move again.

The whole structure swayed back and forth, forcing him to stop after only a few more steps. Eyes shut tight, he paused. Had he assumed too much from the bridge? Would Jefford arrive before he reached the far side? Most vital of all for Stoker, however, was would he even get there?

There was no going back now. He had to push on, testing each step carefully. Around midway he had gotten the hang of how best to tackle the ungainly framework. The second half was much easier and he arrived at the far side sweating buckets but grateful to have reached safety.

Immediately, he secreted himself behind a boulder close to the supporting bollards to await his prey, and none too soon, either. Jefford had made good time up the narrow game run. Stoker watched as his foe approached the bridge, knowing that he also had to make the crossing. An ugly grin split the watcher's warped countenance. 'Come on, you skunk, get your ass out there,' he muttered to himself.

The scout was likewise considering the risks involved. Knowing that his quarry had made it safely to the far side gave him the confidence to press

ahead. This was no time to waste on pointless specu-
lation regarding his own survival. Creaking and
swaying like a drunken cowpoke on a Saturday night
bender, it soon became clear that all his attention
was required to maintain balance.

The halfway point was where Stoker made his presence felt. He stepped out into the open, calling
across to the trapped man. 'Glad you could make it,
Indian-lover,' he hollered jovially. Both hands were
held up to show he was not holding a gun. 'Figure
you can take me from there?' was the sardonic chide,
chilling in its confident expectation of an easy conquest. 'Reckon if'n you try it'll be curtains, don't
you?' The brigand was chock full of confidence.

Wink likewise knew that he could not release his
grip on the supporting ropes. He was stuck fast
between a rock and a hard place with nowhere to go.
The challenger eyeballed his dilemma and once
again hooted with satanic glee. 'Gee, I sure am enjoying this,' he chuckled, removing a large bowie knife
from his belt. 'I could shoot you down right here and
now. But that would be too darned simple.' Straight
away, he began to saw at one of the supporting
cables.

The individual strands soon began to part, causing
the bridge to tremble like a wounded puma. All
Wink could do was hold tight, and pray for a miracle.
Moments later the cable parted. The bridge shuddered as one side collapsed, forcing the trapped man
to cling on desperately to the remaining support.

A couple of buzzards cawed in sympathy but could

offer no help as Stoker turned his attention to the second cable. 'Soon be over,' he called out. 'Say your prayers, sucker. But before you go, take a peep down there at your grave.' The knife was laid across the thick cable, a macabre smirk aimed at the victim attempting desperately to sidle across the intervening span.

They say that your whole life flashes before your eyes when the scythe man comes calling. All Wink Jefford could see was a deep chasm waiting to receive his mangled body.

FOURTEEN

OUT OF THE DARK

All seemed lost. He had tried and failed. Stoker had won. At least he could have the satisfaction of knowing that the rat had been flushed out of his hole. He could not return to Tularosa. And Wink Jefford had been vindicated. Little good it would do him now. Just when the Reaper was about to claim his prize, a light shone bright from the dark tunnel that beckoned.

The cackle of delight spewing forth from the killer's mouth was abruptly cut short. Wink raised his head, bearing witness to his deliverance. The executioner was tottering towards the edge of the ravine. Hands raised with an arrow sticking in his back, it looked like he was appealing to the heavens, but there was to be no spiritual relief. A shriek of anguish issued from the open maw as he tumbled headlong into oblivion. The blood-chilling scream bounced off the canyon walls, fading to nothing as the flailing body raced downwards on its journey of doom.

Barely able to comprehend that some Good Samaritan had snatched him back from the brink, Wink could only gasp audibly, his heart beating a loud tattoo inside his chest. His bowed head rose, searching for the venerable redeemer, and there on a rocky plinth clutching a bow stood the noble outline of Nalin. The captive wife of Mangus Voya had once again saved his life.

All he could do was stare agape at his saviour. The abrupt lurch of the bridge's wobbling remains jolted him back to a grim reality: the stark reminder that he still had to traverse the last section before it gave way. Step by step, hand over hand, he edged along the single remaining strand of rope. Pain-wracked creaks and groans assailed his ears, sounding as if the wounded structure was in its final death throes.

Extreme paroxysms of relief found him scrambling to safety on the far side where Nalin was waiting, and only just in time as the last cable parted. The whole edifice was torn from its mooring, crashing and tumbling into the deep gorge. Regaining his breath, Wink stood up. 'H-how d-did you manage to find me?' he stuttered out.

'This not only crossing of Red Rock Canyon,' she declared in a gruff staccato voice. 'Apaches know of many ways through mountains.'

'Have you heard about Mangus?' Wink enquired tentatively.

Nalin nodded but displayed no emotion at the passing of her husband. 'I watch fight from above

Atoka Springs. He no loss to earthbound life. But Nalin now in worse trouble since his brother Coronadas grab power. I have been forced to flee for my life.'

'What has happened?'

The old squaw rubbed her hands nervously. 'He suspect me of freeing you before but could say nothing while Mangus alive. Without son, nothing here for me anyway. I go to rejoin my people.'

'So why come here to save me? You have already repaid my rescuing of Shinto. And now he has been killed by white men, you owe us nothing.' Wink was truly baffled by the Yaqui woman's action.

'I know in heart, you good man, not responsible for action of others.' Nalin laid a hand across her chest, her tone softening. 'Shinto would want me to help you against real killer.' Wink had more questions but the Indian woman raised a hand. 'This not only reason for offering my help. War between red and white can only end badly for Indian. You man of peace. Can help us find right path.'

Wink shrugged his shoulders. 'I am only one man, and a disgraced one as well. The army won't listen to me now.' He might have been saved from the ignominy of cowardice, but the unjust charge of treason for his actions at Fort Defiance still hung like a dark cloud over his future.

An ardent refutation showed itself in the wrinkled face. Nalin shook her head. 'You are wrong, white man. The tribe are holding son of army chief captive. Coronadas is planning to kill him. Worse still, he will send the man's severed head to fort setting trap when army chief seeks revenge.'

Wink's eyes opened wide. With all this other business occupying his attention, he had clean forgotten the warning revealed by Cracker Jack Torrance. What Nalin had exposed would give him the chance to redress his tarnished reputation while at the same time preventing a full-scale Indian war breaking out. This revelation changed everything. Wink knew that nothing would stop Colonel Dennison from riding out straight into a well-prepared ambush.

'How far is the Mimbreno camp?' he snapped out, the lazy eye flickering like a dancing firefly.

Nalin merely pointed a finger towards the western horizon. 'I take you to where they hold him. You good army scout, able to mount rescue and return army man to father.' The wrinkled look picked up on Wink's uneasiness, mistaking it for hesitation. 'You brave man. Save my son. Not coward like Stoker.' She pulled at his buckskin jacket urgently. 'But we must go now. Execution to be carried out when next sun burns away shadows of night. A tribal offering to gods for success in battle.'

'I was just trying to shake the mush from inside my head.' Wink breathed deeply trying to regain his composure. 'So much has happened in such a short time. A fella needs to weigh things up before plunging in with some half-baked scheme that could easily backfire.' He was thinking about Angie and the others back at Atoka Springs. They would be expecting him to return soon with a prisoner in tow.

Postpone things and they would assume he had failed, and that Frank Stoker was still at large.

But Nalin was right. Not only one life was at stake here. Peace and the safety of many settlers hung in the balance. Mangus was dead but his brother was likely to be just as bull-headed. 'Do you have a spare horse?' he asked.

'No, we must ride double,' she replied impatiently. 'But I know safe crossing of gorge that will bring you back where own horse tethered. Come now, we ride.'

He hauled himself up behind her and they set off along the edge of the ravine, heading upstream. Some way along, a break in the cliff edge revealed a fractured section that had broken away from the main rock face during some mighty land upheaval in times past. It provided a narrow trail slanting down to the bottom of the gorge. Steep and stony, great care needed to be exercised on the tricky descent. But like most of the southern tribes, Nalin was a fine horsewoman.

Expertly, she guided the tough mustang, soon reaching the thin trickle of the creek. Slowly, the severely enclosed ravine began to lessen, eventually fading into the desert terrain. Thereafter it was a simple matter of circling around the lower foothills to locate where Wink had left his own horse. The emotional reunion between man and beast was not shared by Nalin, who viewed horses as mere chattels.

'Come, come!' she urged, irritation edging into her sharp rebuke. Seeing a man greet his horse like an old friend was alien to her nature. 'No time for such foolishness. Much ground still to be covered.'

'Me and this guy have been together a long while.' Wink's measured response was unhurried, patient and precise. 'A man should always treat his horse with the respect it deserves. Patch has saved my bacon more than once and for that I'll be eternally grateful.'

A snort of derision found the Indian shaking her head at the notion that a beast could be addressed by name. She galloped off, forcing Wink to mount up and follow. There was no animosity towards the Indian woman's attitude. He knew the southern tribes would as soon eat a horse as ride it. It was the plains Indians such as the Comanche and Sioux who revered their mounts.

Leading the way, Wink could only follow in Nalin's wake as she negotiated the bleak terrain with easy confidence. The Apaches had lived for generations in this harsh landscape and developed a sixth sense when it came to navigating a course through the labyrinth of canyons and rocky enclaves. The one landmark that Wink did recognize was Church Butte over to his right.

After skirting the edge of the blinding expanse presented by the *Yermo Tierra*, even the great scout himself had lost all sense of direction. Was it any surprise, he pondered, that the Indians had proved to be such formidable adversaries? Negotiating a peace treaty was vital if more bloodshed was to be avoided, but both sides would have to cooperate in reaching an agreeable compromise. Mangus Voya was dead, but his brother was clearly intent on scuppering any deal with the hated white eyes.

The rescue of Lieutenant Dennison was, there-fore, essential to prevent a clash from which neither faction would benefit. Coronadas might well win such a battle, but the war against the infinitely more powerful bluecoat forces was bound to fail through sheer weight of numbers.

They rode all through the night, only stopping to rest their horses and snatch a couple of hours sleep. Wink needed to be fresh in the early morning if he was to figure out a plan of action for the rescue.

And so, as the first flush of the false dawn heralded the start of a new and momentous day, Nalin paused on a rise overlooking the Mimbreno encampment. Numerous wickiups had been erected alongside a creek, nestling in a shallow depression surrounded by turrets of rock: a secret hidden oasis, alien to the arid terrain characteristic of the Sacramento Mountain range.

And there, in the middle of an open sward and clearly visible, was the young officer tied securely to a post. He had slid to the ground, his head drooping. Already the Indians were gathering, their faces painted up ready for the Dance of Death soon to follow. Wink's heart dropped, his broad shoulders slumped. They were too late. How could one man possibly carry out a successful rescue faced with such overwhelming odds?

Nalin read his thoughts when she whispered, 'There is one way to turn this in our favour, but it very dangerous. Demand all of scout's courage and skill.'

143

A puzzled yet hopeful eye urged the woman to continue. 'Anything that will prevent war, I am ready to consider.'

'As wife of old chief, I still have some influence with tribal elders. I will propose a challenge to Coronadas taking over as new chief. It has not yet been agreed by tribal council. Guadalupe has final word. He can permit a trial by combat for your life and that of captive bluecoat. Coronadas will be forced to accept or lose face.' She settled her crystalline gaze onto the scout. 'Is only way. But are you prepared to risk your life in this cause, white man?'

Wink swallowed. He had heard about these kind of trials, but had never participated. Now that Mangus was dead, Guadalupe was much more likely to listen to reason. He responded with a cautious nod, glancing down at the camp where the braves had already begun their victory dance around the pinioned captive. In the middle, a medicine man clad in full ceremonial garb was invoking the support of the spirit world with raised hands.

'We must go,' Nalin insisted. 'When dance ends, captive will be slain. It will be slow and painful, performed by women of tribe.'

Wink shivered. Never had he felt more inadequate. The grim task to which he had consented could so easily end up with him suffering a similar termination. Nevertheless, it had to be done. Adopting a solidly unyielding manner, upright and dignified, and at odds to the churning in his guts, he followed the similarly stoical figure of the Yaqui woman.

FIFTEEN

TRIAL BY COMBAT

Following their humiliating retreat from Atoka Springs, Coronadas was determined to not be beaten. Like Mangus Voya, he was convinced the southern Apache tribes together could overcome their enemies. Peace treaties were an abomination. Numerous ones had been signed before and violated. The only way forward was outright war against the aggressor. And as the new head of the Mimbrenos, Coronadas would hold the answer in their mountain encampment.

The aspiring new chief stood watching the macabre scene, arms crossed. An arrogant leer creased the craggy profile. None of those gathered around him noticed the arrival of Nalin and her white companion. All eyes were focused on the dancers while listening to the impenetrable dirge issuing from the mouth of the medicine man. Only when the duo approached the more substantial wickiup of Chief Guadalupe was their presence heeded. And it was Coronadas who shouted a warning. 'A white eye has entered our camp. Grab him before he frees prisoner.'

Wink was dragged roughly off his mount. His arms were tethered and the six-gun removed. He was then hustled before the main chief, who had emerged in readiness for the final showdown. 'I come in peace, oh brave chief of all Apaches,' Wink intoned in a flat voice. 'I am here to request the release of my compatriot. Killing him will only incur grave anger from great white father in east.'

'Too many treaties have been broken by your people,' Guadalupe's gruff voice rasped. 'The death of this man will send message that Apache will not be defeated. We stand firm against the hated invaders.'

Wink retained a blank expression. But he knew from the surly faces around him that his very survival was in the balance. It was Coronadas who spoke up first. 'Like all white men, Yellow Hair speaks words of false snake. He should join bluecoat dog in death by thousand cuts.'

Numerous other braves echoed the accusation. 'Brother of Mangus is right. All white eyes lie.'

Guadalupe silenced the angry torrent. 'Be silent, my brothers. Let us hear what Nalin has to say. It is she who has led him to our camp.'

Nalin now stepped forward to propose her solution. Back straight as a ramrod, dark eyes glittering like coals of fire, the old woman waited until total

146

silence had descended on the gathered members of her adopted tribe. Even though she was a Yaqui, her position as wife of the dead chief still gave a certain kudos, a tribal status that all had to respect.

'This good man save my son before snake-hearted dog kill him.' Her voice was clear, her testimony delivered confidently. 'Now it is avenged. I trust Yellow Hair to deliver Apache conditions to white chief. It is as he says. Killing bluecoat will bring much death and destruction to Apache. This my proposal. Indian law states captive can gain freedom through trial by combat. I invoke that law. Yellow Hair to fight. . . .' She paused, allowing her next announcement to grab the full attention of the intent crowd. Her finger then swung, coming to rest on . . . 'Coronadas. But only if he has courage of mountain lion, as claimed.' Her eyebrows lifted. It was a challenge for her brother-in-law to concede defeat.

All eyes swung towards the aspiring leader of the Mimbrenos, who was dumbfounded by this unexpected challenge. But Coronadas knew he had no choice but to accept. Refusal would mean dishonour and banishment from the tribe. No true Apache could ever live down that shame.

'What is your ruling, Guadalupe?' Nalin demanded, holding her breath as the chief walked slowly up and down, contemplating the implications of what had been put forward. Everybody present waited with bated breath. For the younger braves, it was something to be relished. The elders were much

147

more cautious. They had experienced much suffering at the hands of deceitful palefaces. But age brings wisdom, and peace was not to be pushed aside as a display of weakness.

'It will be as Nalin decrees,' announced the chief. 'Let each fighter prepare himself for combat.' He then sat down, the elders joining him outside his wickiup.

Coronadas shouldered through the crowd into the middle of the clearing. Bared teeth were on show to display his contempt for the opponent. 'Bring bluecoat here,' he ordered his henchmen. 'Let him watch as I slay Yellow Hair, then send both heads as present for army chief in Fort Defiance.' A roar of approval greeted this suggestion as they untied young Dennison and pushed him across to where the contest was to take place.

The lieutenant had been too disconsolate to notice the arrival and subsequent verbal exchange between the newcomers and Guadalupe. 'So they've captured you as well, Jefford.' His tone was subdued, devoid of the arrogant posturing flaunted at their previous meeting. 'Guess it's curtains for both of us now.'

'Not if'n I have anything to do with it, Lieutenant,' Wink espoused, displaying a measure of confidence he was certainly not feeling inside.

He didn't have time to satisfy the officer's puzzled frown. Willing hands pushed him out into the amphitheatre created by the circle of braves. Most were convinced that Yellow Hair would fall to the cunning and dexterity of Coronadas, a seasoned warrior well used to such hand-to-hand clashes. The would-be Mimbreno chief strutted across to the far side, displaying a proudly supercilious bearing.

In the centre of the combat zone stood a log into which a tomahawk was buried. Both contestants were waiting on Guadalupe to signal the commencement of hostilities. The chief raised a lance. The moment the weapon was lowered the contest would begin. Silence reined over the killing ground, all eyes directed towards the lance.

On the agreed signal, the crowd erupted with gleeful anticipation, urging their chosen fighter to make short work of this foolhardy intruder. Both men launched themselves at the protruding axe. But Coronadas had the edge. Wink knew he would not reach it in time and veered off to one side, avoiding a scything slash by inches as the razor-edged blade whistled past his head.

The Indian spun round ready to deliver the killing blow. But Wink was prepared and grabbed hold of the raised arm. Both men rolled over in the dust. Muscles strained as each battler sought to gain the upper hand. Coronadas managed to break Jefford's hold on his tomahawk wrist. He scrambled away, punching out a growl of triumph that was echoed by his supporters.

'Prepare to meet your end, white dog,' he hollered, charging in to deliver the death-dealing blow. Dennison and Nalin stayed silent, willing the brave scout to counter the lethal chop. Their prayers were answered when the doughty scout ducked beneath the deathly hack once again, grabbing the tomahawk hand and flinging himself backwards. Using an out-thrust foot as a lever, he tossed the startled brave over his head. Coronadas landed with a heavy thud on the ground, the weapon skittering away out of reach.

Buoyed up by the success of the manoeuvre, Wink scrambled to his feet. He snatched up the axe and threw himself on the stunned Indian before he could recover. Sitting astride his beaten adversary, the deadly blade rose to deliver the *coup de grâce*. A stunned silence had fallen across the assembled throng, such was the unexpected twist to the result of the contest.

All held their breath, expectant of the final denouement. Even the birds had fallen silent, watching, all on tenterhooks. The tomahawk fell, slamming down into the ground inches from the loser's head. A gasp went up from the spectators. Nobody present had expected such a finish as the scout slowly rose to his feet and stepped away, turning his back on the vanquished Indian.

In a loud voice, strong yet edged with prudence, he proclaimed earnestly, 'Noble braves of the Apache tribe, I, Yellow Hair, have no wish to slay my brother Coronadas.' He held out a hand, a peace offering, which the Indian regarded with bewilderment before accepting the gesture. 'There has been too much killing already. Too many harsh words and thoughts have passed between us. The time for a lasting peace should be grabbed by both our nations. Allow me to return bluecoat warrior to his father and I promise to use all my power to urge the white leaders to meet with Apache elders to work out a treaty that will last for all time.'

It was a speech thought out on the spur of the moment. But its resonance struck deep. Muttered imprecations filtered through the gathering as braves discussed the startling finale of the confrontation. They were all impressed with the scout's bravery and courage, not least Coronadas, who was the first to speak up. 'Yellow Hair has proved beyond doubt that he is truly a great warrior. He has cleanly defeated me in combat, but I hold no bitterness against him.'

All now looked to Chief Guadalupe for his judgement. 'By showing mercy to his foe, Yellow Hair has won the greatest of victories. Coronadas also has demonstrated deep wisdom by accepting defeat like a true brave. As chief of all Apache tribes, I keep word. You are free to return with bluecoat to fort. And none shall stand in your way.'

Wink had one final request to make before departing. 'I wish for Nalin to accompany me so that she can take passage for return to her people. Will Guadalupe grant this plea?'

'Is this your wish as well?' the chief asked the anxious squaw.

A nervous nod preceded the stammered reply. 'I-it is, great chief. Now that husband is gone to join son, Nalin want to pass final days with own tribe.'

The craggy face of Guadalupe, a feast of channels scoured by the desert winds, remained set in stone as he considered the request. Once captured, it was rare indeed for a captive to gain release except by the defeat of the tribe. But the aging chief was growing tired of constant battles with the white invaders and yearned for peace. 'Go then with Yellow Hair, and may the Great Spirit grant you peace. Two of my braves will guide you through mountains to main trail.'

A palpable relaxing of tension settled over the encampment. But for Wink Jefford there would be no respite until he had escorted Lieutenant Dennison back to Fort Defiance. 'It's vital we start out immediately,' he said to the mightily thankful young officer. 'Every day that passes with you absent from the fort is likely to encourage your father to start a war. If'n that happens, all this will have been in vain.'

SIXTEEN

REUNION AND REDEMPTION

The two escorting warriors, now conspicuously devoid of war paint, left their charges on the edge of the Sacramento Mountains when the trail from Carrizozo came in sight. Without a word having been spoken, they turned around and rode off.

'Shucks, Wink,' Dennison exclaimed, wiping sheen of sweat from his face. 'Am I glad to be shot of those guys. One minute they're after carving me up into strips of meat, the next I'm free as a bird. And it's all your doing. I don't know how to thank you enough.'

'The only thanks I need, Lieutenant, are for you to urge the Colonel to reconsider any armed insurrection against the Apaches. The only way for the settlers to live in peace is for a lasting treaty to be negotiated. Otherwise, we're in for a blood bath the like of which we've never seen before, and heaven only knows how that will end.'

'I'll do my best, Wink,' Dennison assured his escort. 'The old boy is a stubborn critter, but he ain't stupid. Once he sees that I'm safe and well and learns of your part in the rescue, he'll soon come round. I'll make darned sure of it.'

The two men and the Yaqui squaw pressed onward. They still had a stiff journey ahead of them. There could be no stopping until they reached the fort except for the necessities associated with bodily functions. Eating and drinking were done on the hoof from emergency army rations carried in Dennison's saddle pack. It would have to be enough to sustain them.

After passing Church Butte, Wink's heart skipped a beat when he came upon the remains of the wagon train, the once proud conestogas now just a heap of blackened bones littering the desert floor. Dennison pointed them out, unaware of the discredit that had been heaped on his associate. 'Let's hope we can come to an agreement with the Apache and put an end to carnage like that,' he remarked. 'At one time I would have wanted nothing more than to avenge this with more bloodshed. Your wise counsel has changed my mind. I'm sure if both sides get together, a harmonious compromise can be reached.'

Wink muttered in sympathetic accord. But all he wanted was to distance himself from the harsh memories engendered. Relief flooded his taut frame when the young officer did not suggestion a detour to inspect the devastation. On they rode, surmounting the Capitan range on their third day. Descending through the pine-clad foothills, the plateau lands were soon traversed. Wink looked behind to see Nalin close behind. He was impressed by her resilience. No sound of complaint had been forthcoming; she had maintained the relentless pace with stoic determination.

Eventually, and with some trepidation, the small party found themselves approaching the wooden palisade of Fort Defiance. Both men were praying that no armed band of troopers had yet been despatched to exact a brutal revenge for the assumed death of Lieutenant Isaac Dennison. It was now over a week since the young officer's capture. His father was bound to have received word of the fate awaiting him, and worst of all, the grizzly package heading his way.

Would Colonel Dennison have retaliated in the only way he knew? Or showed circumspection to await developments? Wink was cynically inclined towards the former, but earnestly prayed for the latter. The nearer they came to the fort, the more tense Wink became. On reaching the gates, he was in the lead. The sentry on guard duty recognized him immediately from their previous encounter when he had allowed Shinto to escape. His gun rose as he stopped the three arrivals.

'You're under arrest, Jefford,' he snarled. 'And this time there won't be any reprieve. The Colonel will throw the book . . .' The threat tailed off when he spotted Lieutenant Dennison behind. 'W-what the heck. . . !'

'It's all right, Trooper, we're together,' the officer interjected. 'Is the colonel still here?' All the stunned sentry could do was point a tremulous hand in the general direction of cavalry headquarters.

The two men left him open-mouthed. Others were equally nonplussed as the arrivals drew to a halt outside the office building. They stamped into the main office without knocking. Dennison jumped to his feet, all ready to browbeat the intruder. His jaw dropped a mile on seeing his only son safe and well. He was too startled for words. A tear strayed down his cheek, which was brushed away immediately. 'Is it really you, Isaac? H-how did you escape?' he burbled, coming round the desk and grabbing his son in a bear hug.

That was when he noticed the scout standing in the doorway: yet another totally unexpected surprise. But this one brought a dark scowl to the commandant's face. 'What in thunder are you doing with that traitor?' he snapped, once again adopting the unbending stance of a hard-bitten Indian fighter.

The lieutenant soon calmed his father down with a full explanation of recent events. 'So you see, Dad, if'n Wink hadn't put his life on the line, I'd have been thrown into a ravine and my head alone would have come back here.' He paused, gesturing for Wink to step forward. 'And by showing mercy, he was able to convince Guadalupe, the big shot in charge

156

of the whole Apache nation, that coming to an agreement regarding land boundaries is the only way forward.'

Wink held out his hand to the strong-willed officer hoping that he would reciprocate. 'I shouldn't have gone against your ruling by allowing Shinto to escape,' he apologized. 'I know that now. But I was so sure his arrest would cause a whole lot of worse trouble with the Indians.'

Dennison's hard features remained rigidly tight. Then he nodded, a softening around the deep-set eyes indicating a change of heart. 'I have to admit that I've been too mule-headed in the past. I could have been more accommodating when it came to negotiating peace treaties and keeping them.' He accepted the mollifying gesture, reaching for a bottle of Scotch on his desk. 'What say we all have a drink?'

The atmosphere in the office was now significantly warmer than the last time Wink had stood there. 'I'll leave you to arrange a meeting with Guadalupe, Colonel,' Wink said, knocking back the drink quickly. 'I need to go visit some folks who will be figuring I've let them down again.' Puzzlement creased Dennison's leathery features. 'It's a long story, Colonel. I'll tell you about it when we have more time. Just that it concerns a woman.'

The older officer chuckled. 'I might have guessed a dame would be involved in this business somewhere.'

'And that reminds me,' Wink added. 'I owe my life twice over to a Yaqui squaw. She's waiting outside.

Could you arrange passage for her back to her tribe?'

'Leave it with me, Wink, and I'll make sure she travels first class.'

A final handshake and the meeting broke up. Much as Wink would have liked to get back on the trail straight away, he knew that Patch needed to rest up overnight. He was plumb tuckered out as well. A good night's sleep and some proper food would set them both up for the journey on the morrow.

That night, as he settled down for the first decent sleep he'd enjoyed in a coon's age, the exquisite features of Angie Henstridge kept impinging on his subconscious thoughts. The Colonel was assuming he would return to Fort Defiance and resume his role as chief scout, but Wink had other ideas. He was hoping that Angie would join him in bringing them to fruition. And that silver strike would provide the capital to invest in their future cattle ranching enterprise.

It was three days later when he finally crested the same ridge offering the view of the Running W section. This time he was mounted on his own horse. Patch snickered, also appearing to recognize it. Corby Wishart would know where Angie had decided to settle down. He pressed onward, and arrived at the ranch house to find Wishart still engaged in general maintenance work, this time fixing broken fences.

On spotting the approaching rider he dropped his tools in shock. 'I'd given you up for lost, boy,' he said. 'We waited around a spell before figuring either

Stoker or those darned Apaches had done for you.'

'Neither one, Corby. And Stoker's dead. Killed by a friendly squaw.' Wishart scratched his head, unable to comprehend the mind-boggling assertion. 'Ain't got time to tell you the whole story. I need to see Angie.'

'That gal was cut up when you didn't return.'

'Where is she staying?' Wink asked, eager to depart.

'Her and Rachel have gone to live at the Stoker cabin. It ain't much of a place. That's why Frank was trying to borrow money off'n me until he could dig up enough silver.' He tutted at the notion of how the varmint had taken possession of the land. 'Since we ain't seen hide nor hair of him, we all reckoned he skipped the territory to avoid a lynching.' The older man then went on to give directions on how to find the cabin. 'Good luck to you, young fella. Although I don't figure you'll need any of that.' A sly wink accompanied the hearty chuckle as Wink spurred off.

Late afternoon shadows were crawling across the landscape when the lowly cabin hove into view. Wink slowed Patch to a walk. Just then, a woman came outside and began pumping water into a bucket from the well. It was Angie. She paused, shielding her eyes from the setting sun. The job was forgotten when she recognized the straw hair beneath a tan plainsman.

A cry of exhilaration brought her sister-in-law to the door, but Angie had eyes only for Wink Jefford.

Dismounting, Wink ran to meet her. He swung the girl off her feet, twirling her around before planting a kiss on eager lips. It was a melding of pure ecstasy that neither wanted to end. No longer was there a dark shadow hanging over them. The sun had emerged, pointing to a brilliant future.